EARL B. PILGRIM

DEDICATION

To Bob,

A special thanks goes to a good friend, Robert (Bob) Ropson, who gave his support and much encouragement for writing this story of Sir Wilfred Grenfell.

Bob is a crab fishermen and member of the Long Range Search and Rescue Team.

Bob is someone who always puts others first.

At this time Bob is receiving treatment for cancer at the Roddickton Hospital. I would like to wish him a speedy recovery.

All the best,

Earl

Earl B. Pilgrim

THE DAY GRENFELL CRIED

*Grenfell's compassion brought him in conflict
with powerful fish merchants and almost broke his heart*

Library and Archives Canada Cataloguing in Publication

Pilgrim, Earl B. (Earl Baxter), 1939-
  The Day Grenfell Cried / Earl B. Pilgrim.

ISBN 978-0-9781496-9-7

1. Grenfell, Wilfred Thomason, Sir, 1865-1940--Fiction.
2. Newfoundland and Labrador--History--Fiction.
  I. Title.

PS8581.I338D385 2007   C813'.54   C2007-902362-2

Cover design and layout by Diane Burke Lynch

Printed in Canada
by Transcontinental
2007

DRC Publishing
3 Parliament Street
St. John's, Newfoundland and Labrador A1A 2Y6

Telephone: 709-726-0960
Email: staceypj@nfld.com

TABLE OF CONTENTS

CHAPTER 1

Battle Harbour

Mother and daughter were picking bakeapples (cloud berries) on Caribou Island, just across the tickle from their home in Battle Harbour, when they saw a small two-masted sailing sloop coming into the harbour with its sails fluttering in the light westerly wind. They knew it was not a fishing schooner; it was sleek and nicely painted and they could hear the sound of its engine.

An hour later, they were rowing home in their leaky punt.

"Mom, hey Mom," the hollow cheeked daughter spoke in an unsteady voice as she paused from bailing water with a puncheon (wooden bucket). The girl's eyes were glued to the shoreline as they drew nearer.

The mother, as thin and bony as her daughter, became more alert as she sat gripping the oars with calloused hands.

"What is it, my dear?" she asked as she pulled on the oars.

"There's a couple of men standing on the beach near the co-op store where we've got to go ashore…do you know them, Mom?"

"I'm not sure, but I think one of them looks like John Croucher," her mother answered as she strained her eyes to get a better look, noticing at the same time that the strange sloop was docked at the head of a nearby wharf. "Yes," she added, "one of them is John Croucher, but I don't know the other man, he don't look like someone from around here. I think he's a stranger. "

"There's another man standing at the head of the wharf and he's looking at us too, Mom," her fifteen-year-old daughter said with concern in her voice.

The older woman looked in that direction again, but continued to row on towards the beach.

"Do you think they wants us, Mom?" asked the girl.

1

The mother looked at her daughter, then at their raggedy clothes, and said with a grin, "I wouldn't say that they wants us for very much, my dear."

The mother and daughter were the Greens of Battle Harbour, Labrador. They were clad in long, dark dresses that were literally hand-me-down rags. They had been out picking bakeapples for twelve hours; bent over on the damp bogs in the blazing sun, battling black flies and mosquitoes, with nothing to eat only hard bread and cold water. With empty stomachs they were now returning with their day's harvest, on their way to the Mission Store to trade for something warmer to wear or food to ease their gnawing hunger pains.

Saying nothing more, Mrs. Green rowed the punt on toward the shore as the two men on shore watched intently.

The tide was out at this time of the day, revealing slippery, jagged rocks covered in green seaweed.

The punt was about twenty feet from shore when its keel touched the bottom, stopping it in over a foot of water.

Mother and daughter stood up, ready to step ashore. They looked at the men standing on the beach in front of them.

"Good day, ladies," the stranger said politely.

"Good day, sir," said Mrs. Green.

The stranger, who was wearing a pair of long rubber boots, walked out near the punt, placed his hand on the gunwale and looked down into it.

"I see you've got two fine looking buckets of bakeapples there," he said.

"Yes, sir. This was a pretty good day picking, there was a lot of flies, but except for that it was all right," Mrs. Green said in a tired voice as she stood holding one of the oars in her hand.

The daughter looked nervously at the distinguished looking stranger, and then at her mother.

"Are you selling those berries, ma'am?" the stranger asked.

"No, sir," Mrs. Green replied quickly.

"Why not?" he asked as he looked her straight in the eye for the first time.

"Yes, we are selling them," interjected the daughter.

"How about selling me five gallons? asked the stranger as he continued to look at the mother. "You will still have five gallons left to sell to someone else."

"No, sir," said the woman. "They're not for sale."

The daughter spoke up again, "Sir, we are selling them, but to the Mission."

"To the Mission?" said the stranger. "But why not sell them to me?"

"No" said Mrs. Green.

The stranger looked directly at her. "How much are they paying you at the Mission for a gallon of bakeapples?"

"Forty cents a gallon," the woman replied.

"I'll give you 70 cents a gallon and I'll take the whole ten gallons, that's seven dollars you'll make."

"No, sir, we are going to sell them to Mrs. Grieve," the woman said after a moment's thought.

"Who is this Mrs. Grieve?" demanded the stranger.

"Mrs. Grieve gives out clothes to the poor people, she's the doctor's wife," answered John Croucher in a mocking tone of voice.

Croucher was the Battle Harbour agent and store manager for fish merchant Walter Baine Grieve, owner of Baine Johnston and Company Limited. St. John's-based Baine Johnston had purchased the Battle Harbour fishing premises in 1871. The company owned all of the large buildings and the wharf near the beach where Croucher and the stranger were standing.

"So that's what's up, hey John?" said the stranger as he looked at Croucher.

"Yes, that's what is happening," Croucher replied.

By now the stranger was red in the face. "Come on, madam, sell me the berries," he said as he turned to the woman again.

"No," she said in a voice that left no room for argument.

"How will you get paid for these berries?" he asked angrily.

"Mrs. Grieve will give me a slip for the berries and I will take the slip to the clothing store and get our clothes for the winter, which will be much more then the seven dollars you are going to give me," the woman replied curtly.

The loud voices were beginning to attract attention and it was then the Greens noticed another man walking along the beach toward them. He was also from the sloop. He was a big man, well dressed and obviously not a fisherman. Hearing what was going on, he was coming over to get his five cents worth in.

"So, this is what Grenfell's crowd is doing, John," he said as he drew near. "I make no wonder the co-op is getting all the business."

The man had one hand on his hip and the other in his coat pocket. The Greens noticed the shiny gold ring on his finger.

"Don't you know who I am?" he said.

"I don't know, and I don't give two damns who you are... and what's more I'm not going to sell either you or him my berries and that's that," said Mrs. Green.

The big man was about to tell her he was the Minister of Fisheries for Newfoundland, but she continued her angry tirade.

"Sirs, let me ask you something. In December month, if we're out of food, as we used to be before the co-op store and Dr. Grenfell's crowd came here, will you be around then with your money or food? You weren't here when people were starving, and in January or February if people get sick and need a doctor or nurse, will you come around then with your money and your fancy schooner?"

No one spoke.

"No, sirs," she said, "you'll be in your comfortable homes and shops in St. John's while people down here are suffering with sickness and cold."

She looked at the man with the gold ring and he put his hand in his pocket and tried to hide it.

"I came from Northern Newfoundland and it's the same thing back there," she said with anger in her voice and her eyes blazing. "Before the Mission came, the people were all in your hands and almost starved to death; everyone was in rags and it's only now that they got a bite to eat and clothes to wear. You're all fish merchants. I can tell by the gold rings and nice clothes and the way you got your hair combed, and I wouldn't sell you any berries to save your life. You had your chance but you robbed us blind, so now get out of our way."

With that, she stepped backwards and stumbled out of the boat and into the Labrador Sea. The young girl screamed when she saw her mother disappear over the side. One of her mother's rubber boots hooked onto the wooden pin that was on the gunwale of the boat and left her with her legs sticking up in the air and her upper body under water.

The man with the gold ring quickly jumped into the knee deep water and grabbed the furiously floundering woman by her shoulder. Using one hand, he tried to lift her up, "Take it easy, madam, take it easy," he said.

"Take it easy," she mocked as salt water streamed down her face and her voice boomed out all around the harbour. "Get out of my way and let me go," she yelled, using language not becoming either ladies or gentlemen as she coughed up seawater. Another man helped her stand up. "Get out of my way and let me go," she repeated as she cursed and kicked.

"Are you all right, madam, are you all right?" asked the men.

"No, I am not all right," she said as she gasped for breath and then suddenly attacked the two men, punching one in the face and almost knocking him down, and clawing the other's face.

As they turned to run, she held on to them and screamed to her daughter to throw the hand-gaff to her (a hand-gaff is a stick with a sharp steel hook on one end used for taking big fish out of the water), but luckily her daughter refused.

The men tore themselves loose and ran toward the sloop, leaving her shaking her fists in anger. As she struggled with the men, she noticed the one she grabbed by the face had only one hand, but that made no difference to her.

This was Battle Harbour, Labrador, on August 5, 1916.

CHAPTER 2
Arch Piccott

This had not been a good day for Archibald Piccott. He was the Fisheries Minister for the Colony of Newfoundland and Labrador, and he didn't like getting punched in the stomach and having his face clawed by a woman he thought was out of her mind.

He was upset and angry as he walked into Baine Johnston's store and steadied himself along the counter with his one hand. Piccott, who was born in Cupids, lost one of his hands in a mishap at age fourteen.

(The Honourable Mr. Piccott was on a working pleasure trip along the coast of Labrador, more or less taking inventory of the premises owned by his colleagues in the House of Assembly, and catching a few sea trout and char along the way. It would be nice to give them a copy of his report stating all was well when he got back to St. John's, as this could justify his use of the government-owned Fisheries patrol boat, *Petrel*.)

The skipper at the time was Captain Kennedy. He'd been with Piccott on the beach. (He would go on to be the navigator onboard the ill fated S.S. Viking, which blew up off the Horse Islands with a large loss of life in 1931.)

Piccott, Kennedy and Croucher soon began to talk about what had just happened on the beach. All had been fine on the lovely August day when the *Petrel* tied up at Baine Johnston's wharf and John Croucher came out to meet them.

After handshakes and a short conversation, Croucher and Piccott went to the company office.

As they walked along the wharf, Piccott asked if there were many bakeapples around, and said he'd like to buy a few gallons. Croucher said berries were plentiful and people had been picking them for more than a week.

"Look," he said, pointing to the punt coming across the harbour with two women in it. "They should have a couple of gallons of bakeapples to sell. They're just coming from the berry bogs over on the island and for sure they've got some." "Good," said Piccott, feeling in a happy mood.

And now, as Minister Piccott steadied himself just a few minutes after his encounter with Mrs. Green, he was not a very happy man. He was, in fact, in a terrible rage and cursed and swore as he wiped blood off his face with his handkerchief. "I've never seen or heard talk of the likes of this before," he bellowed.

"No more did I," said Captain Kennedy, who was equally shook up. "You talk about a vicious woman."

"She struck me in the mouth twice and clawed my face," said Piccott.

"We're lucky to be alive after that run-in," said Croucher.

"You were right about what's going on, Croucher," said Piccott. "Can you imagine what they're doing with all that charitable stuff they're bringing in…do you know if they're paying any duty on all those big bundles of clothing they bring into the country from the States in the name of charity?"

Croucher wasn't sure, but feeling the Fisheries Minister was looking for something to sink his teeth into he replied, "You know full well there's no duty paid on that stuff, sir. It's like the rifles and ammunition they had come in a while back, they sold them, and that was what some American had given them to give to the people down here free of charge."

"They're at everything according to that," said Piccott as his mind went back to a court case he'd heard about a couple of years ago.

"This woman kept referring to a Mrs. Grieve, who is she?" he asked.

"She's Dr. John Grieve's wife," said Croucher.

"That's it, now I remember...I heard some of the Customs officers talking about the court case here at Battle Harbour where Magistrate Penney got afraid of that Grieve fellow and left."

"That's only small stuff," said Croucher, knowing he had the Minister upset and wanting to keep him that way.

"Keep talking, Croucher," said Piccott, as he took out a notebook and began to write.

"If there's not a stop put to this co-op racket, every business along the Labrador Coast that's operated by fish merchants like us will be put completely out of business. After all the good we've done for the people down here over the years they ignore us and flock to the co-op."

"I'm going to do something about it, John, you just watch and see," said Piccott.

"The Grenfell Mission is the cause of it all," said Croucher, knowing this was the time to get even with Dr. Grieve for starting the co-op store in Battle Harbour.

"This is one time Grenfell and his bunch are going to jump because I'm going right to the Prime Minister the minute I get back to St. John's and call for an investigation and have the whole works kicked out of Labrador," said Piccott as he once again wiped his bleeding face.

This was the best news that John Croucher had heard for a long time. "*What a stroke of luck,*" he thought, and almost spoke aloud. "*Old woman Green attacking the Fisheries Minister over a few berries was more than I could hope for in years, maybe, just maybe, Grenfell's co-ops will get squashed and we can continue on as before.*" He had a job to keep from laughing out loud.

CHAPTER 3

Red Bay

T he little fishing village of Red Bay, Labrador has experienced many ups and downs since the first Basque whalers came there in the early 1500s.
Thousands of men and women have occupied this land since that time, battling poverty and hardship, trying to keep body and soul together in the midst of sweat, hunger and tears.
Most left behind not a trace or memory.

It was the 10th of July 1896 when the small hospital ship, *Sir Donald,* carrying medical missionary Dr. Wilfred Grenfell dropped its anchor in the muddy bottom of Red Bay harbour.

The afternoon was clear and sunny, and the small town was busy, with fishermen cleaning and salting codfish at every stage head around the harbour.

Once the anchorage was secured and the canvas folded and tied, the crew lowered a small boat to take Grenfell ashore.

Everyone knew the small schooner called the hospital boat. Dr. Grenfell had made several trips here before, holding medical clinics in people's homes and handing out clothes and food to women and children. But this trip to Red Bay was different because the people were expecting him. He was here now for more than a medical mission.

Since he first arrived in Labrador in 1892, he'd been watching what was happening between the fishermen of Red Bay and the fish merchants and he was convinced that somehow something had to be done.

Dr. Grenfell knew the plight of the people. He knew how hard they toiled for a living, he knew they brought in a lot of fish, but yet they were close to starving. He said there was only one word that he could use to sum it all up and that was "oppression."

Wherever he went, in every little village and outport, it was the same. The people were in rags.

He stated in his writings that the only thing he could compare it to were the leftovers of the slave trade.

He said too that, "the sod huts of Ireland were mansions when compared to most of the houses along the Labrador Coast at the time."

There was nothing in the way of medical attention for the people along the Labrador Coast. It was available only in the far north where the Moravian missionaries had stations among the natives.

The system worked in such a way that early in the spring, depending on the ice conditions, the merchants would arrive on the coast in their large schooners.

It was said that as these merchant schooners got close to each little settlement the agent or merchant aboard would speculate how many men had died during the winter.

They wondered if it was even worthwhile going in with supplies; their only concern was a labour source.

Onboard the vessels they had supplies for the fishermen who would sell to them, all on exchange basis, no cash was involved.

A five-dollar bill did not exist along the Labrador Coast and the same went for the Northern Peninsula of Newfoundland.

In places where many fish were caught, the merchants would build large stores and summer living quarters for the staff they brought with them.

The dreadful way it went was if a fisherman would not take his fish to the merchant who had the food and supplies then he would go without food and supplies. It made no difference if the fisherman and his family were starving, they would get nothing.

The so called "truck or credit system" of business gave the merchants all the advantages, especially when hardly anyone they were dealing with could read or write.

Dr. Grenfell said that if there was to be any hope for the people along the Labrador Coast or Northern Newfoundland the credit system would have to be crushed.

Some fish merchants had permanent stations built along the coast with managers running their business, while others operated from large vessels and were known as "floaters." Usually, the captain of the vessel was the business manager, and sometimes he was also the merchant.

Some fish merchants had on shore fishing stations spread out along the Labrador coast. These merchants would have fishing skippers and a crew of men go to certain places near the fishing grounds and erect temporary shacks and catch and salt fish. Women and children and elderly men who could no long fish accompanied the crews and did the job of making or curing the fish; washing the salted fish and spreading it on flakes to dry in the sun. This they did for twenty-five cents a quintal (112 pounds).

People going to Labrador making fish went aboard the mail coastal steamers heading north. They were herded into the hatches of these ships with dogs, hens, sheep, and often a couple of cows, as well as their gear for the summer. They had to cook their own food where they slept. For sanitation purposes, they used buckets and pails that were dumped over the side of the ship twice a day. Animal urine and droppings were cleaned up as soon as it arrived on the floor.

Moses Harvey, Head of the Anglican Church in Newfoundland, heard of the atrocities and took a trip to Labrador on one of these mail steamers to get his own first hand look and see if what he'd heard was really true.

On his return to St. John's, he wrote about the trip, saying what he saw could not be described in words. He wrote a full report and gave it to the Newfoundland government but nothing was done; his report was ignored. This is what caused Harvey to go screaming to the British government demanding an investigation be carried out, and saying if nothing was done he would take the matter up with the international community. England responded by sending Sir Francis Hopwood to investigate.

What Harvey saw on his trip down to Labrador was nothing compared to the return trip these people made back in the fall. It is impossible to give the reader a true picture of what really went on in only a few paragraphs. Justice could only be done if a complete book was written, however, one incident does give an example.

The second year Dr. Grenfell came to Labrador he had with him a young physician by the name of Dr. Eliot Curwen. Grenfell wrote about it this way:

It was sometime around the first of October when we were in the fishing village of Indian Tickle. We arrived in the steam launch, *Princess May*, just as a storm was coming on. We were there only a few minutes when a large schooner arrived with a trap boat in tow, on its way south. It was very low in the water, indicating it was fully loaded, as it came close to us and let its anchor down. After the wind came up to almost gale force, we saw another schooner enter the small harbour. It was also fully loaded and had two boats in tow, the waves were flushing the decks. It came close to us and anchored.

Some of our crew recognized them as the floating merchants out of Conception Bay who were operating further north with fishing skippers, and crews of men, women and children curing the fish for market. We noticed a lot of men on the decks of these schooners.

It was a nasty evening, with wind and rain, which caused us to stay aboard or launch. While we were having tea, we heard someone calling to us. One of our sailors responded and told us that a man from one of the schooners was looking for a doctor. He said his wife was very sick and he would like for us to come on board to see her. Of course, we went immediately.

When we got near the vessel, the captain did not seem to be very happy. He stood back and did not welcome us aboard as was the custom wherever we went. We thought it strange.

The man told us his wife was down below deck in the hatch. We were not surprised at hearing this because we had already seen a lot of unusual conditions in the two years since coming here. The man led us over to the open hatch. We noticed a lot of men standing around, watching in silence. I saw that the captain had moved away, out of sight. We suspected he must have gone below to his quarters.

Near the hatch, just below, were two lit lanterns that were giving off a lot of smoke and a terrible stench. It was obvious they were burning cod oil to supply the yellow flame.

We were told that the sick woman was on the left side of the boat as we looked toward the rear.

The husband jumped down into the hold and beckoned us to do the same. When I looked down, I was surprised at what I saw. In the centre of the hatch were the tops of several barrels and we suspected they were put there for stepping down into the hatch.

I estimate it was not more than two feet between the cargo below and the deck above. As I looked in through this dark, narrow channel, I could see eyes staring at us through the dim light.

The husband took one of the lanterns and asked me to follow him. Lying down on his side and holding the lantern with one hand he lifted himself with his other elbow and used his legs in a bicycle motion to push himself along. There was not enough room to kneel up and crawl.

We immediately realized we were crawling on some kind of nets because just near me were cork floats.

As we slid along, I saw women and small children lying down and watching us silently; no one smiled.

We arrived at the side of the sick woman who appeared to be suffering from claustrophobia. She was unable to get her breath and just beginning to have signs of a high temperature. We also noticed she was pregnant. When we asked how she felt, she complained about pains in her chest and back. We wanted her to come aboard the *Princess May,* but she refused, saying she only wanted God to spare her life long enough to get off this floating death trap and get home.

We examined her and found no signs of difficulty with her pregnancy. She was suffering from fear of being stuffed in between piles of salt codfish and a deck that creaked every time the vessel rolled in a swell.

We gave her medicine and told her husband to keep her warm and dry and try to get her outside once in a while for fresh air and exercise. He promised he would try.

After we left the woman, we started back to the open deck, the husband leading with his lantern.

As we got near the hatch, we could smell a terrible stench. It was unbearable. I asked what it was and the man replied it was the cod oil that was stored in barrels below the dry fish. "Sometimes the barrels burst open if there is a big sea heaving," he said, adding, "But what really stinks the most is the barrels of blubber we have in the hold. The skipper has that for feeding the dogs we have on the back deck."

We were glad to get back on deck again to get fresh air. I wanted to talk to the man privately so I said we wanted him to take us back to our ketch as we had medicine to give him.

We took him down below on the *Princess May* and questioned him about his voyage to Labrador. He told us they had spent all summer at the fish, salting, washing it out and spreading it on the flakes and rocks until it was dry. He said they hoped to go back home on one of the coastal steamers but were told it cost the merchant too much, so they would have to go on the schooner when it came to collect the fish and cod oil. "After they straightened up with us," said the man, " they started loading the cargo aboard."

We asked him how he got paid, that is, if he received any cash. He hardly knew how to answer because money was out of the question. He said they got paid in food and had it aboard with them now on their way home.

He said after the cod oil was loaded aboard, then came the salt bulk fish (heavy salted fish, not dried), and then the dry fish. A large tarpaulin covered everything. The cod traps and nets went in on top of this if there was room to spread them out. The women and children crawled in on top of the nets and spread their blankets on the traps. Some men took a duck feather bed for their wife to sleep on if there was room to squeeze it in between the cargo and the deck. The vessel we had been on had no ventilation in the hold, and the hatch had to be kept off at all times for fear of everyone smothering. We asked the man how much they got paid for their work and he said twenty-five cents a quintal (112 pounds) for dry fish. In other words, if they dried two hundred quintals of fish they shared fifty dollars between five people. This year, they were told they would not get any part of the money made on cod oil.

We asked why the captain avoided us when we came aboard his vessel, and he said the captain hadn't wanted to take passengers on board in the first place for fear of an accident on the way home, but the agent forced him to take everyone. He said he guessed the captain didn't want to meet us for fear of getting his name spread around.

The man told us he was frightened almost out of his mind for his family and the rest of those aboard. He said there were sixty people stuffed in the two foot gap below deck. Frightened children screamed every time the vessel rolled, people were vomiting all over the place, especially the young children. Vomit was running down through the nets and it was unable to be cleaned up, causing a terrible stench. "I just don't know how we are going to be able to make the trip home. It's a ten day voyage," he said as he put his hands to his face and wept.

While we were talking to the man, one of our sailors came and said we were wanted on deck. I came up and saw a small boat near the side of our vessel. The man in it wanted a doctor to come aboard the other schooner and see his sick infant.

We were curious to have a look aboard the other vessel and told him we would come right away.

We launched one of our own boats and rowed to the schooner where the captain welcomed us aboard and shook our hands. We were led straight to the hatch and told where to find the mother and child. The stench here was worse than on the first schooner. I got down and looked in under the deck. I didn't think there was room for me to get in there.

Dr. Curwen decided to crawl into the mother and child. He only got a short distance when he was told they would pass the child out to us; this they did by passing it from one to another. It was a six-day-old infant. When we examined the baby we found it had a disease of the mouth called Thrush. We treated the infant then passed it back through the same channel to be with its mother who was lying on a bag of duck feathers for a mattress.

I looked around at this unspeakable mess; it was obvious the deck was leaking because buckets were hung from the deck below to catch the rainwater that was now dripping down in several places. We could tell the schooner was old by the rotting wood around the hatch. We wondered what conditions were like when the seas broke over the deck in a storm. On deck, just above the area where women and children were housed, twenty dirty mongrel dogs were penned up. Day and night, the dogs were continually barking and fighting. While we were there, we saw two men trying to clean the dogs' urine and droppings by using water and birch brooms; the stench from that alone was unbearable.

We spoke to the captain after treating the patient. He said he was frightened and feared for everyone on board but he had no choice. He said it would never change.

Dr. Grenfell had arrived in Red Bay on his first trip of the year in mid-June of 1896. After talk he'd heard the previous year about the oppression of the fish merchants, he wasn't surprised to see what was happening.

He knew the people living there had all that they could take and were about to make their move. As his small rowboat neared the wharf belonging to William Pike, a fisherman he knew well, he saw boxes and crates stacked high. Pike, his son, and many other men had gathered on the wharf.

Grenfell noticed their solemn faces as they stood waiting for him to get out of the boat.

"William," he said," what's going on?"

William Pike was an honest, hard working fisherman, and one of the few in Red Bay who could read and write. He looked at Grenfell with tears in his eyes.

"We're all leaving, Doctor."

"Leaving... you mean leaving your town, going away?"

"Yes, sir, we have been in contact with the government of the United States and they've agreed to let us go and live in the State of Maine." Grenfell didn't know what to say as William continued, "Last winter most of us almost starved, if it hadn't been for an American banker (a large schooner that fished with trawls offshore) that came in here in a storm late last fall with food aboard, we might have."

The other men nodded in agreement.

Dr. Grenfell knew the men were right, but to see them leave their homes and their country without a fight seemed like a cowardly thing to do. A thought flashed in his mind. He had seen it before, in England, Ireland, and in many parts of India and Africa.

Wherever the merchants had control over government, oppression was the order of the day. It was no different here in Newfoundland, and what he had seen in the last four years was cruel beyond all description. But now, he was facing the reality of it.

He knew there would be enemies created by what he was about to do, and that would have long-term effects on his medical mission, but he knew it had to be done.

"William," he said, "I want to call a meeting and it's not concerning medical problems. I want every man in town to come to the meeting."

William Pike was surprised to hear the doctor make such a statement. He knew that Grenfell was going to tell them something important, he could tell by the tone of his voice.

By now, a large crowd was gathering and Pike knew that there was no trouble in getting everyone to attend.

"Yes, Doctor," he said, "I certainly will have everyone attend a meeting; we can meet in our fish store."

Turning to the crowd, he shouted, "Men, I want you fellows to quickly go around town and tell every man to come to my fish store. Dr. Grenfell is calling a meeting."

Red Bay was one of those places where a lot of fish were caught. A merchant from St. John's had a large business established there. He had a wharf big enough to accommodate a large schooner. He also had warehouses and a retail store. The manager, Joseph Penney, also from St. John's, lived comfortably in the company house. Penney was educated to the point that he used to teach school in an outport on the Avalon Peninsula, but he gave it up to work as an accountant with one of the large fish companies.

The company soon promoted him and sent him to Red Bay to manage their business. This company operated solely on a barter system. It was, as the people would say, a take out and turn in operation. This meant that people who couldn't read or write took goods and merchandise from the merchant's store in the spring without having any record of what they had taken. In the fall, they turned in their dried salted codfish with hopes of getting supplies for the winter.

If, however, the voyage was bad and few fish were caught and the fisherman never squared up his bill at the end of the season, his family would have a very lean winter and no mercy was shown. There were always many people in this category, having to rely on the kindness of their neighbours to keep them alive.

When Dr. Grenfell first came to the Labrador Coast he found this practice to be rampant. In letters to the Newfoundland government he stated that disease took second place to oppression and starvation everywhere merchants were involved in the fishery or the fur trade.

Grenfell was fully aware that if he was to realize his dream of a successful medical mission for the people of Northern Newfoundland and Labrador, he had better not step on the toes of the fish merchants because they were the ones running the government. However, he knew that people's survival and health depended on his success and for this reason he decided it was time to make his move.

It took less then an hour for every man and many women to be crammed into William Pike's fish store.

It wasn't every day that someone as important as this English physician showed up in their town and requested a public meeting. When Grenfell entered the building, the people were silent as they stared and listened.

Dr. Grenfell was quite an orator. In several conversations with the Reverend Stanley Hancock and Dr. Baxter T. Gillard, who chaired several of Grenfell's meetings, they told me it was quite an experience to see him in action, giving a lecture or speech.

He began this meeting by thanking William Pike for bringing everyone together on such a short notice. With that said, he quickly came to the point.

"There is no doubt, ladies and gentlemen, that we are facing an emergency here at Red Bay, and not only here at Red Bay, but all along the Labrador Coast and on the Northern Peninsula of Newfoundland.

"I have watched conditions here in horror, especially the way the fish merchants are robbing the people," he said as he carefully picked his words. "In order for me to carry on my medical mission successfully things have got to change, and let me say this, it can't get any worse. If any change comes it has to be for the better unless the whole population dies of starvation. This is supposed to be a civilized country, but what I have seen since I came here is nothing short of slow genocide on the part of a group of fish merchants who are running this Colony."

Dr. Grenfell went on to tell the audience about Ireland and England and what had been done to correct the situation there.

"There is only one way to stop these mad men from robbing us and that is for us to control the sale of our own fish products ourselves," he said. "The way to do it is what the fishermen did in England and Ireland, and that is form a cooperative business and run it yourselves."

A woman by the name of Ryan, tall, in her thirties and dressed like a man, stood up. Everyone cheered.

"Listen, Doctor," she said. "I'm the one behind the idea of moving away from here. You said it right, Doctor, there is no use us trying any more, the fish merchants have trampled us under their feet for too long and we're not going to take it any longer, at least I'm not. I've read about cooperative stores and been telling the people here for years that we should start one. Maybe they will listen to you."

Glad he had the support of this woman, Grenfell then made his statement. "We will start a co-op store here at Red Bay. It can be done and I am the one who knows how to do it."

He asked for a show of hands to see if the people were in favour of forming a co-op. Everyone raised their hands.

William Pike spoke up. "But we're all packed and ready to move away from here, Doctor."

Grenfell was quick to answer. "Unpack your things, men, you're not going anywhere. You don't have to go; this is June now and prime fishing time. By the last of August you can be selling your catch to the market yourselves."

Everyone was excited and anxious to know when and how this could be done. Dr. Grenfell gave them full details how a cooperative organization had to be set up and managed.

He knew because he had been involved in helping to get several started in England before coming to Newfoundland.

Cooperatives originated in England in the 1840s and the fundamental principles were: open membership; democratic control (one share, one vote); distribution of surplus to members in proportion to their transactions, and limited interest on capital invested in the cooperative.

"I have to go down north to attend to patients, but I should be back here in about a month, depending on the ice conditions. Today, I will write the Prime Minister informing him what we intend to do," said Grenfell as everyone stood up and cheered and clapped. "Now go and unpack your trunks and crates. You're not going anywhere. In the meantime, go out and set your traps and start fishing again, I will arrange for someone to come here with supplies to keep you going through the summer."

With this, he adjourned the meeting and everyone shook his hand and thanked him as they left. Dr. Grenfell then went from house to house attending to the sick.

CHAPTER 4

Red Bay Co-op

And now, on the afternoon of July 10, Dr. Grenfell again called a public meeting in the local school that stood on rickety tree trunks in a grassy meadow in Red Bay. The people were expecting him and had great confidence he would save their town. Of course there were a few connected with the fish merchant who were not happy to see him arrive. (Twenty-one years later, on October 3, 1917, William Pike was summoned to a court hearing in Forteau, Labrador. He gave a complete report on the meeting that Dr. Grenfell held at Red Bay when he organized the first cooperative store in Newfoundland.)

Out of all the people in Red Bay, only fourteen could come up with $5, the cost for each share, and one of those was the local midwife, Aunt Minnie Pike. In other words they could only raise $70; there was not another cent around.

One young man, due to be married in August, had contributed the $3 his father had put away to pay the Bishop after his father said, "The co-op, my son, is the most important. You can always get married."

After every cent in the town was brought to Grenfell and counted, he formed a committee.

William Pike was elected as secretary-treasurer and also as manager of the newly formed co-op, with a five man elected board of directors. Grenfell said he would put $1,000 of his own money into the co-op, a loan to get it started. He said he didn't want any interest on his loan.

(It is important to jump ahead in this story for a moment and say that between 1906 and 1911 the Red Bay cooperative store paid Dr. Grenfell back his loan of $1,000, and gave his Medical Mission a gift of $300 in appreciation of what he did for the people of Red Bay. The Red Bay co-op also helped finance another co-op in West St. Modeste, a neighboring town to the south. This information is taken from the recorded testimony of William Pike in 1917.)

Following the July 10 meeting, Dr. Grenfell and Aunt Minnie Pike were called to a home on Penney's Island, in Red Bay Harbour, where a young child was very sick.

An examination showed the child had a bean pushed up into its nose. It was not an easy task to remove the bean, however, after a considerable amount of time, Grenfell, with the help of the old midwife, managed to extract it without resorting to an operation. While they were at the house a man came with a message for Dr. Grenfell, requesting he come to the store of the local fish merchant, which was managed by Joseph Penney.

Grenfell sent word he would come as soon as he could. He listened as Aunt Minnie warned him there could be trouble and said he should have someone accompany him.

"I don't need anyone with me," he assured her.

She said Penney was a very arrogant man and had told several people if a co-op was started in Red Bay there would be trouble for Dr. Grenfell. Penney said if a co-op was started anywhere on the Labrador Coast, Grenfell wouldn't get away with it. The fish merchants said they would cause trouble for him from then on.

Dr. Grenfell asked the midwife to sterilize his used instruments in boiling water. He closed up his medical bag and asked her to wait at the house while he went to visit Mr. Penney.

As Grenfell neared the store for his meeting with Penney, he was uneasy and unsure of what to expect.

He noticed that several of the local men who had earlier been at the meeting were watching him.

He was in no mood for an argument, or any kind of confrontation. However, if anyone wanted to have a discussion about reasons for starting a co-op, he was certain his side of the debate would win out.

He had no idea what type of person Penney was, and had only heard he was loose with the pencil when it came to squaring accounts.

Going directly to the door, he opened it and walked inside. A man of about thirty was standing inside the counter. He was clean-shaven and sharp looking, wearing dark pants held up by suspenders and a black and green shirt.

"Good afternoon, sir," Grenfell said in his pleasant English accent.

"Ahh, good afternoon, Doctor," said Penney, immediately recognizing Grenfell who, in turn, was quick to place his St. John's accent.

"You must be Mr. Penney, the company agent."

"Yes, I'm Joseph Penney, and you must be Dr. Grenfell."

"Yes, I am, and how do you do?" said Grenfell, holding out his hand. Penney gave Grenfell a warm handshake and came out from behind the counter.

"Well, Doctor, I've heard you're a very busy man along the coast of Labrador."

"Yes, I am. There's a lot of work to be done, it seems every time you turn around someone is sick and has a problem. I feel we are only scratching the surface, just a band-aid compared to the larger picture."

"I know," said Penney.

"How much do you know about the Labrador Coast and the people who live here?" Grenfell asked him.

"I know everything about around here," said Penney.

It was apparent to Grenfell that Penney either didn't know very much about the goings on, or that he did not want to talk about it. "Last year," he said to Penney, "there were 20,000 people who came from the island of Newfoundland and fished along the coast of Labrador. If you add those 20,000 to the people who live here all year round the numbers would be very high.

"And the horrible thing about this is that there's only one doctor and one nurse, along with a half dozen midwives, to give medical services to all these people. We haven't got time to eat or sleep when we come into coastal water."

"I know, I know," said Penney, pointing to a chair and inviting Grenfell to sit down. "I was told to come here by one of your employees. He said you wanted to talk to me," Grenfell said very politely as he thanked him and sat down.

"Yes," said Penney as he nervously looked out through the window. He cleared his throat. "I'm the agent for this firm. This is a large firm and the main supplier for this area."

Grenfell was quiet as Penney continued, "We've been here now for over twenty years. I've been here for ten; this is my tenth summer at Red Bay. Our headquarters are in St. John's."

Grenfell nodded. "We, or I, have tried to be very fair to the people of this little town and the surrounding area," said Penney. "Now mind you, I haven't given the people everything they wanted, you know how it is; we're not in the land of milk and honey."

Grenfell sat tight-lipped as Penney rolled a pencil between his fingers. "You can't let people run you Doctor, or you would have nothing. I've been handling someone else's goods, you know, but I've been very fair."

"Mr. Penney," said Grenfell, "I am a medical doctor for the Mission to Deep-Sea Fishermen and I have been here now for four years. I haven't tried to be fair with the people, Mr. Penney, I have been fair and completely honest with everyone I've come in contact with. I've given them everything they were entitled too, all of my time, all of my medical knowledge, and all of my expertise. The people with me have done the same."

Penney listened as he continued, "The people didn't want to ruin me because I gave them what was due them and what they were entitled too and even more."

Penney was going to speak but Grenfell held up his hand and went on, "You said this is not the land of milk and honey and that might be true. I don't think the people along this coast, Mr. Penney, are looking for milk and honey, or mansions with flower gardens. The people living along this coast and the twenty thousand that come up from Newfoundland every summer are only looking for what's due to them. They want justice done for what they earn."

Penney walked to the window and looked out before turning and staring at Grenfell with anger in his eyes.

"Dr. Grenfell," he said. "Can you imagine the word 'justice' and do you know we have had people's names on our books for over twenty years because they're unable to pay their bills? Some are just barely able to keep themselves afloat. Look at all we have done for them. We help them with their boats; we supply their fishing gear and keep food in their stomachs."

Penney stopped talking and waited for Grenfell to reply.

The doctor looked into Joseph Penney's eyes and visualized the fear he had put into the hearts of poor souls he'd dealt with over the years, people who tried to get their rights while straightening their account at the end of the fishing season.

However, Penney should have realized he was not dealing with one of those poor souls now.

"Sit down, Mr. Penney," Grenfell said very quietly. His response was not what Penney expected to hear. "There is a currency in this country called money, and for this reason I would like to ask you a question," said Grenfell.

Penney sat down.

"Have you ever settled an account for anyone and paid any balance due with cash in the past ten years?" Grenfell asked a silent Penney. "I know men here who have been fishing since they were boys and now have grown sons fishing with them and they tell me they've never seen a coin in their whole lives; all they know about is rope, fish hooks, grub, and your company."

Penney pulled his chair over to the counter and put his clenched fists on top. Grenfell was a master at lecturing and knew how to deliver his remarks in the most effective way.

"I bet the only money the people around Red Bay have ever seen is in your name, and a 'Penney' is as low as you can go in the line of currency," he said as Penney slammed a fist on the counter. "You listen to me, Doctor!" he said, almost yelling. "Ever since the last time you were here, there have been a whole lot of arguments and discontent around this settlement. The word co-op is poison to the fish merchants and especially to agents like me. You know what human nature is like; people will jump for anything, especially fishermen."

"Mr. Penney, I have been coming to the Labrador for four years and in all that time I've never yet met a fisherman who was independent; they are owned by the fish merchants. They are slaves, Mr. Penney, and slavery is supposed to be outlawed. If this was in Abraham Lincoln's day and he sailed up the coast of Labrador and talked to the people he would immediately declare civil war on the fish merchants for what they are doing to the people of Labrador. They're no different then the black cotton picking slaves that Lincoln freed, and you know it. You spoke about justice a few moments ago, Mr. Penney. Let's you and I go over to that window and have a look around, please."

Grenfell walked to the window and beckoned Penney over. "Have a good look around and tell me what you see, Mr. Penney." Penney looked at Grenfell then back again at the town before clearing his throat. "Well," he said, but before he went any further Grenfell spoke again. "Do you see any prosperity? Or anything that even looks like it? For the love of God, Mr. Penney, take a look at the houses, most of them are just hovels, yes, just hovels covered with mud and sods wrapped around a wooden frame, and heated with stoves that they made themselves."

Grenfell looked hard at the agent.

"Look at the faces of the women and children over there," he said. "They're pale from the lack of nutritional food. Their faces are long and drawn from the lack of something to laugh about. Just look at their clothes, they are all but rags with patches on top of patches. Mr. Penney, there are people here who can't even afford to mark the graves of their dead. What a pity."

Grenfell pointed to the waterfront. "Just look at the boats tied to the wharves, they're little more then a bunch of slabs nailed together and covered with tar. That is what they use to go out to sea and bring in your fish."

Penney knew he was telling the truth, but he had to be loyal to the merchant; they had taught him that loyalty was the best policy.

Grenfell spoke again, "For just a moment you and I should compare the real facts."

He pointed to a sod hut that hugged the side of a little hill not far away. "Look at that hut over there, I bet you know that family. I would say the people there have worked their lifetime fishing and your company undoubtedly has taken every fish they've caught, and everything they've worked for. That man is now waiting to die."

"What's your point, Doctor?"

"My point is that while the people down here perish, the fish merchants live in mansions and dine on luxuries."

This was too much for Penney. "Just a minute, Doctor Grenfell, just a minute. Before you go, I want to ask you something."

"Go ahead," said Grenfell.

"Do you know what a co-op will do to this business? It will completely destroy us. The fishermen are saying if one is started we won't get another fish from them and they won't buy anything else from us. If that happens, this business will be finished. Some fishermen are even saying now they're not going to sell us any more fish."

"That's not true, Mr. Penney. When the co-op gets started, all you'll have to do is undersell it and put it out of business. But the only thing is that you will have to use cash and keep good records instead of handing out a little and taking all."

"I will remind you one thing, Grenfell, if you start this co-op in Red Bay, you will regret it."

"What does that mean Mr. Penney?"

"I don't think you're a stupid man, Dr. Grenfell. You know full well that the government is mostly made up of fish merchants or their sons. They're the elected representatives. They're the ones that make all the decisions for everybody, and they're the ones that can stop you."

Grenfell was about to question Penney but he continued, "If you start a co-op and put me out of business, Doctor, I will never forget it as long as I live. And let me tell you something, both of us are on a long road and there's no doubt our paths will cross again. I have friends in high places and I will use them to fight you."

"I see," said Grenfell. He knew that Penney could be a dangerous foe and that he wanted him to leave his store. He walked to the door then turned and said to the business agent, "This afternoon we organized the Red Bay cooperative store and will be commencing business immediately."

"Fine," said Penney, "I will write company officials in St. John's and let them know."

"Very good, and I thank you for your time," said Grenfell.

As he stepped outside, he noticed a crowd of men gathered not far from the store. They were all shareholders of the co-op. He saw smiles on their faces, the first smiles he'd seen since coming ashore in Red Bay.

CHAPTER 5

More Co-ops

I n 1903, Dr. Grenfell started another cooperative store at Indian Harbour, Labrador. Soon after this, and after hearing about the great success of the one in Red Bay, almost all of the fishing towns along the Labrador Coast and around the northern part of Newfoundland wanted to start a co-op. It was 1903 that really saw the cooperative expansion. One old timer said every time a new one was started it was another nail driven into the coffin of Dr. Grenfell because the fish merchants were out to get him.

Grenfell was concerned, but his Mission was moving ahead in leaps and bounds and he had the people behind him.

"This is what the people want, and this is what the people will get," he said to Rev. Moses Harvey when he was in St. John's that fall. He knew there would be repercussions when he started interfering with the fish merchants. But the Reverend Harvey was also a thorn in the side of what he called 'the fish merchant government.'

Grenfell now began to visit people who lived far up in deep bays along the Labrador Coast, people who made a living trapping and living off the land. What he found was appalling. The trappers and their families were almost one hundred percent illiterate. And he discovered the same practice was going on with fur buying as with fish buying.

In one incident alone, he found a fur buyer had offered a trapper $15 for a prime silver fox. Grenfell stepped in and stopped the sale. He took the same fox fur and sent it to a fur buyer in the United States who paid the trapper the grand sum of $150 for the silver fox. Of course, this created quite a stir between the trappers and the fur buyers in Labrador.

Between 1892-1912, Dr. Grenfell made an amazing difference to people's welfare. He built hospitals, nursing stations, schools, libraries, orphanages, and industrial schools. In 1908, he introduced reindeer from Norway to the Northern Peninsula. He started a pig-breeding farm for people around the coast. He brought in prime sheep breeding stock and distributed young lambs to families who wanted to raise sheep. He ran agriculture courses that helped people grow larger and better crops of vegetables. He also introduced the fishermen to better fishing equipment. He built a large sawmill at Roddickton and established a large vegetable farm. He built a sizeable dock at St. Anthony where schooners could be taken out of the water and repaired. He built a hotel at St. Anthony, sent a Labrador orphan named John Newell to the States to learn the hotel business, and then sold the hotel to him at cost price. Best of all, he helped the people organize themselves and start cooperative stores.

Grenfell was also a lecturer. From the very beginning, he went to the United States and lectured at universities and great halls of society, including Carnegie Hall and the Metropolitan Opera house in New York. He also went to London, England, and to most of the cities throughout Europe, lecturing and recruiting doctors and nurses. He created quite a stir worldwide. The impact was so great that people in many countries started donating money, clothing, goods and even large boats to be used as hospital ships. Newspapers around the world carried stories about the work Grenfell was doing in Labrador.

In 1912, Dr. Grenfell started the International Grenfell Association. This was a charitable organization dedicated to caring for the sick and helping the poor, and Grenfell put together a board of directors made up of many prominent people.

To Newfoundland fish merchants this doctor who could get audiences with kings and queens, presidents, prime ministers and sheiks was an enemy who had to be thrown out of Labrador, and that was mainly because of the cooperatives he'd started. He could either pack his things and leave voluntarily or they would force him out.

CHAPTER 6
John Grieve

In April of 1906, Dr. Grenfell was giving a lecture in an auditorium at the University of Edinburgh. He told his attentive audience about the work he was doing with the Royal National Mission to Deep-Sea Fishermen in Newfoundland.

Afterwards, he walked around shaking hands and was introduced to a young man by the name of John Grieve, who had been a practicing physician in Edinburgh for two years.

Grieve was so impressed with the lecture given by the Labrador doctor on his work in North America that he was immediately recruited. In May of 1906, he came to Newfoundland with Grenfell.

As they traveled across the Atlantic, Grenfell and Grieve made plans for their future work. Their goal was to not only provide first class medical care, but to educate the people. They wanted to change Newfoundland's economic system and for that people had to know reading, writing and arithmetic. They needed to be educated so fish merchants or any other traders wouldn't be able to take unfair advantage of them.

According to reputable sources, before Dr. Grenfell came, there were no visits from any doctors along the Straits of Belle Isle. Reverend J. T. Richard, Anglican minister of Flowers Cove, said the only Newfoundland government doctor who ever visited was a Dr. Fisher who was sent from St. John's for a day or so during the terrible diphtheria epidemic.

People in the cold, northern climate suffered terribly from lack of proper clothing and housing; there are photographs of makeshift huts where families lived all along the coast. But the greatest problem was the lack of nutritional food to help fight off disease. Dr. Grenfell pleaded for proper food and supplies to be made available, especially for children and mothers.

"It's a different matter if the people weren't working, that would be an excuse, but just look at what's happening. The people are producing an excellent fish product in abundance. It's being exported to help feed the world but they are not benefiting anything from it," he told a group of clergymen in Boston when he gave an outline of what he was encountering along the Labrador Coast and the Northern Peninsula.

The Reverend Dr. Moses Harvey had negotiated with the officials of the Mission to Deep-Sea Fishermen in 1891, and arranged with them to have a doctor sent to Labrador after he saw first hand the lack of services to the people along the Labrador Coast. When officials headed by Sir Francis Hopwood came to St. John's, Harvey told them he was sure there was nothing in the world that could compare to the terrible suffering and hardship going on in that area. He was very concerned too when he saw how Newfoundland fishermen and their families, along with dogs, sheep and goats, were herded into the hatches of mail steamers going north. The trip could be as long as a week as they headed for the tar papered shacks and sod huts that would be their summer homes along the rocky shores of Labrador.

On their trip across the Atlantic, Grieve and Grenfell talked about helping the people organize cooperative stores so that they could run their own lives and buy what they wanted. Grenfell said there was no doubt they would have to appeal to the citizens of the United States for assistance in getting cooperatives up and running. He said he could ask for money, clothes and equipment at lectures he gave in the States. If clothes were donated, he said, people would have more to spend on food.

CHAPTER 7
Harry Locke Paddon

Before proceeding further, it is very important to have the reader meet another one of the colorful pioneers who came with Dr. Grenfell in 1912 and spent the rest of his life helping make a better life for the people of Labrador.

This was Dr. Harry Locke Paddon.

Paddon was from England. As a boy he was taken to one of Dr. Grenfell's lectures, and from then on his aim in life was to become a medical doctor and join Grenfell in Labrador.

After studying at Oxford and obtaining his medical degree, he went to the North Sea as a physician to a trawler fleet, which is where he learned navigation and seamanship. In 1912, he was recruited by Dr. Grenfell and came to Newfoundland ready to work up north.

Grenfell sent him to a small medical facility at Indian Harbour, Labrador, for his first season. Paddon said he "saw it all" at Indian Harbour and was more than prepared to take on the challenge of helping Dr. Grenfell make changes.

In the fall, when fishermen and their families left Indian Harbour and returned home to the island of Newfoundland for the winter, Dr. Paddon moved to the head waters of Lake Melville where there was a group of small settlements made up of mostly trappers and guides. Seeing the conditions people were living in he became very concerned for their welfare. The result was he settled in the trapping village of Mud Lake and established a medical clinic there.

Shortly after Dr. Paddon came to Labrador and took over the hospital at Indian Harbour, the Governor paid him a visit, accompanied by Dr. Grenfell. Perhaps to help justify the spending of public money, the Governor swore Paddon in as a justice of the peace shortly after he arrived. Most of the fish merchants said this was a mistake, that the Governor should have never made Paddon a justice of the peace, especially after he had attacked their activities and said they were not giving the fishermen a square deal.

In his capacity as a justice of the peace, Paddon wrote to the government requesting someone come and investigate the "goings on," as he called it, between the fish merchants and the people buying furs in Labrador. He received no reply to his request.

Paddon said the worst illness in Labrador was malnutrition. He said he was having problems curing other diseases because people, especially the young, were undernourished due to an improper diet. He said it was very difficult being a doctor treating people who were malnourished. His thinking was the same as that of Dr. Grenfell.

While Dr. Paddon was at Indian Harbour, a young nurse from New Brunswick, Canada, by the name of Mina Gilchrist came there to work with him. The two fell in love and were married in 1915. They later moved into Lake Melville and vowed they would make a change both medically and humanly for the people of Labrador.

(In later years, their son, William Anthony (Tony) Paddon, who was born in Indian Harbour in 1914, became a physician. He served in the Royal Canadian Navy during the Second World War, and then joined the International Grenfell Association in St. Anthony where he served as assistant medical officer. In 1947, he took over operation of the hospital in North West River that his mother had been running almost single handedly since his father died in 1939. Tony Paddon retired in 1978. In 1981 he was appointed Lieutenant Governor of Newfoundland and Labrador, the first Labradorian to hold the post.)

CHAPTER 8
St. Anthony Headquarters

During the winter of 1896, Dr. Grenfell received a letter from a man named Ruben Simms in St. Anthony, Newfoundland. Grenfell had met Simms the summer before when he was anchored in St. Anthony harbour doing a clinic on board his medical schooner *Sir Donald*.

Simms said he was writing on behalf of everyone in the community and in the surrounding area. He appealed to Grenfell to come to St. Anthony and set up headquarters there.

"This town is considered to be located in the best harbour in Northern Newfoundland. The water is deep and anchorage is good with plenty of room for a large number of vessels," he wrote. He went on to say that the community was located at the tip of northern Newfoundland making it a jumping off place to Labrador, and was also the centre of the cod fishery on both sides of the Northern Peninsula. He said the climate there was better then most places in the area.

"There's lots of timber for building material close to the harbour and plenty of good fresh water in rivers nearby," he wrote. "I own a large section of land located in the center of the community that consists of fifty acres."

Simms said if Grenfell was willing to come to St. Anthony and make it his base of operations he was willing to give the doctor and his Mission to Deep-Sea Fishermen the title of all his land, free of charge. He said too that men were willing to volunteer their time to build a clinic on the land.

"People are perishing from total neglect such as proper food, clothing and medical attention, and not taking into account the greatest need of all, education," wrote Simms, ending with a heartfelt plea, "We need you, Dr. Grenfell."

When Dr. Grenfell received this letter he was elated. He said many times afterwards it was the first bit of good news he had received since he arrived in Newfoundland.

Grenfell immediately wrote Reverend Moses Harvey and asked him to forward a letter to Simms saying he was prepared to accept his offer. It was late in March of 1897 before Simms received the letter saying Grenfell was looking forward to seeing him when he returned in the spring.

That summer, people of the St. Anthony area built a medical clinic for Grenfell. It was constructed mostly of slabs, the seams were corked with moss, and the roof was covered with the sails from an old schooner.

Simms made the windows out of lumber he took from the side of his own house, and they were large enough to provide plenty of light. Grenfell used this building for more than two years before coming up with plans for a hospital. The Mission to Deep-Sea Fishermen paid men to cut and saw logs into lumber for the hospital building. This was the first time most had seen money in their lives.

Grenfell was surprised to discover he could get men in the immediate area to do any jobs that needed to be done, even though none were trained in specific trades. After being shown once, the men became carpenters, plumbers and electricians.

When Grenfell asked how it was they had done such a rough job on building the medical clinic, Simms replied, "We made sure that when you went to the States or England looking for money to build a hospital, the photograph of the one you were now using would not look like a mansion." Grenfell laughed with amazement at the wisdom of these men.

When the hospital was finished, Grenfell immediately organized a cooperative at St. Anthony and Ruben Simms became the director.

There are many stories told about Dr. Grenfell and how he organized ways for fishermen to get more money for their catches of fish. An old gentleman by the name of Charley Bessey of Cape Onion, a small settlement on the tip of the Great Northern Peninsula, told me the following story:

"We grew up in a little settlement and were full fledged fishermen when we were ten years old. My father had a big fit-out, that is he had a lot of fishing gear," said Uncle Charl, as we all called him, before lighting his pipe and settling back for a yarn. "Father brought in a lot of fish. He used to have up to ten men some years. Some years he would get over 2,000 quintals of codfish, but the sad thing about it was we would never see a cent of money. We would only get grub (food), clothes and fishing gear for the fish. One day we were putting away a load of fish when Dr. Grenfell came into our little settlement and dropped anchor. Well now, this was a big thing. We knew it was him because his schooner was different from everyone else's, you know, kind of squarely built like a tub." Uncle Charl laughed. "The next thing we saw was a punt rowing in toward our stage head. Someone said that the person sitting in the back of the rowboat was Dr. Grenfell. He was the talk of the coast, everyone was anxious to see him. Everyone stopped what they were doing and watched as they got closer. The two men came to the stage head and sure enough it was Dr. Grenfell. He shook hands with everyone there, youngsters and all. 'I would like to speak to the man in charge,' he said after he got up on the wharf.

Uncle Charl blew smoke over his head and continued.

"Father spoke up and said, 'I can't say that I am in charge, but I'm the first one to get out of bed in the morning, Doctor.' Grenfell laughed at that, he liked wit. Father and the doctor left the wharf and went up to the house. Of course we were all very excited; we could hardly do any work. After a while Dr. Grenfell and his assistant left our place and went around from house to house doing medical work or whatever he used to do.

When Father came back to the stage he was looking kind of happy. We knew there was something up, you could tell. After the fish was all put away he called everyone together and told us that Dr. Grenfell had said there was a ship coming in sometime this week buying fish and that she was from Canada.

Canada was no different than the United States to us then, because we were used to seeing Americans all the time, especially the crowd working with the Grenfell Mission.

Father told us that the Canadians were going to pay double the price the fish merchants from St. John's were paying us, and they were going to give us cash.

This was a big thing; we had hardly seen a piece of money in our life let alone Canadian money. We were all wondering what it would look like.

A couple of days later a big boat came in the harbour. You could tell she wasn't a Newfoundland boat. She was different from what we were used to, kind of high and wide, and clumsy looking. When she got anchored, Father went out to her and got aboard. She was out of Montreal, so they said. The Skipper asked if they had any dry fish to sell. We had some, not much, but we had over a thousand drafts of salt bulk fish, (this was fish that was heavy salted and went directly to the European countries). If we had all of our fish dried we would have made a fortune, because they paid us $8 a quintal (112 pounds) for what dry fish we had. They paid us $6.50 for a draft, and that was 200 pounds. So you can make it up yourself, it was $6,500 because we had a thousand drafts. We also had $500 dollars worth of dry fish. Father had $7,000 in dry cash, as they say, all in Canadian money. We never saw the like before. The sharemen who were with us had never seen any money before.

The Canadian boat almost got a full load of fish right here in our town. Well, certainly, the likes was never known before around here. I had a pocket full of change. We couldn't spend it because there was no store only up around St. Anthony and that was a full day's steam away in motor boat. We used to go around jingling the money in our pockets especially where the girls were.

Father had it all planned about what he was going to buy when the floating merchants came. But he got the devil's surprise when they came." Uncle Charl started to laugh.

"The merchant's agent from the schooner came ashore to our wharf, I can see him now. He was a big man with curly hair. He got up onto the wharf and asked father how much fish he had to go aboard. 'Not one fish,' Father replied.

The agent thought he was joking at first, but then he realized that Father was a man who never joked about things like that.

The agent knew we had got a lot of fish because he could see all the piles of cod's heads and sound bones on the bottom. He looked at Father then said, 'You're after getting a lot of fish that's for sure, where did it go?' Father looked him straight in the eye then replied, 'I sold every fish to the Canadians who were here last week.' The agent looked at us in shock. 'I don't believe you,' he said.

Father knew he could not take it all in. 'Come in the stage and have a look for yourself,' Father said.

The agent went in and had a look for himself and sure enough the salting stage was empty except for what we had salted within the last few days. The agent got mad and asked, 'What? Did he pay you all cash?'

Father looked at him with kind of a grin on his face and said, 'Yes, all $7,000 was in green backs.'

'I'm going to have the last laugh,' said the agent.

We didn't know what he meant at the time, but when Father asked him if he would sell us some food we knew then that he had us where he wanted us.

'I wouldn't sell you a cake of hard bread to save your life,' he said. 'Go buy it off the Canadians. They're the ones that got your fish, so they're the ones to give you the grub.'

He was starting to walk off the wharf when Father stopped him. 'Just a minute before you go out to your schooner, I got something to tell you,' he said, and the agent turned around and asked what it was in an unpleasant way.

Father said, 'It's no good for you to go anywhere in this harbour because every fish here is sold and gone, so you might as well sell us the goods you got aboard rather than take them back to St. John's. You'll still make a profit on the stuff you got aboard.'

That really made the agent angry.

It was then he realized someone had educated us about what the merchants were doing. He was as quiet as a fox. He calmed right down and then asked, 'When was the doctor here, I mean that fellow, Dr. Grenfell?'

Father was quick to reply, 'Just over a week ago I think.'

Well, that was enough to make the agent go crazy.

'Now I know the reason why that Canadian boat came in here,' he said. 'Grenfell had her come in here to take all the fish where we wouldn't get it. He's been at the same thing over in Red Bay.'

'Never mind that foolishness,' said Father. 'Don't you realize that the times are changing?'

'Time's are changing,' the agent roared, 'the times haven't changed for us.'

Father said, 'We got paid in green backs so you might as well sell us our winter supply.'

'I wouldn't sell you one ounce of anything to save your life,' said the agent.

Father then asked the man to quietly leave the wharf and he did. After he had gone Father called everyone up into the store loft, where we used to pack the dry fish while we were waiting to ship it. Everyone was concerned and asking what we were going to do now. Well, no one spoke. Here we were with a whole lot of money and couldn't spend a cent, at least not around here. But Father was smart. Now I don't know if Dr. Grenfell had told him what to do or not, but he had it all planned.

'Don't worry about a thing, men, I know what we will do,' he said. We all looked at him wondering what he was going to say. 'There's lots of food and anything else that you want to buy over at Red Bay,' he said. 'They have a co-op store over there and there's one at Flower's Cove too.'

Of course, this was out of the world as far as we were concerned. Father started to make plans to go to Flower's Cove so the next week we went there, not only us, but almost every boat in the settlement went and came back with all our supplies for the winter and we still had plenty of money left over, thanks to Dr. Grenfell. He opened our eyes because from then on when the fish merchants came in to buy fish they had to have cash in their hands."

Uncle Charl was laughing when he finished his story. He was like a young kid full of glee.

CHAPTER 9
Grenfell's Idea

D r. Baxter Gillard of Englee, Newfoundland, a small fishing community on the east side of the Great Northern Peninsula, told me the following story about how Dr. Grenfell was not afraid to campaign anywhere for a better way of life for the people:

"When I was eighteen years old I became manager of the large fishing firm John Reeves Limited of Englee, Newfoundland. We bought most of the fish caught in the White Bay area. We were like all the fish merchants around the coast at that time, take in and take out. There was no money involved, all credit.

One evening when I went home to my dinner, Father told me there was a public meeting scheduled for 7 p.m. at the Orange Lodge. He said Dr. Grenfell was there and was holding a public meeting he wanted all the men to attend.

I went to the meeting and the place was packed with almost every man in town. Rev. Stanley Hancock chaired the meeting for Dr. Grenfell. Stanley sang 'God save the King,' and the meeting got under way.

Dr. Grenfell started talking about the hard times around the coast and down around the Labrador. It was heart wrenching and we knew it was true. He went on to talk about the cooperative stores that were established at Red Bay, Labrador, and Flowers Cove in the Strait of Belle Isle. He told the people our company in Englee was robbing them. Naturally, all the people at the meeting agreed with him. Now, as I was the manager of the company, everyone turned and looked at me. I wasn't going to sit still and let this go by without having something to say.

I jumped to my feet and said, 'Dr. Grenfell, you are telling lies, what you're saying about our company is not true. I'm the manager of John Reeves Limited and I know what's going on.' After I made that statement I sat down quickly and was quiet. There was such a silence in the hall you could hear a pin drop.

'Who is that man?' asked Grenfell.

The chairman whispered to him, 'That's Baxter Gillard, he's the manager of the fish company here at Englee.'

Dr. Grenfell asked me if I would stand up. I replied, 'I will stand up if you will retract your statement.'

'Statement retracted,' said Grenfell.

I stood up, but my legs were shaking. He quickly asked me if I would be interested in becoming a member of an improvement committee for the town. I told him that I would be interested but I would have to talk to my boss first. Dr. Grenfell accepted that. That was when I became involved in community affairs but not in any cooperative. "

In early June 1913, Dr. Grenfell was on a medical patrol of the Labrador Coast. The ice had moved off early and he made a dash for the hospital in Indian Harbour.

When he got in the Sandwich Bay area he decided to start doing clinics in the 30 or so small places where people lived through the winter. He said later that what he saw was so horrific it could not be described in words.

When he arrived in Indian Harbour he was pleased to see that Dr. Paddon had arrived from North West River for the summer and had the hospital open. Paddon was getting ready to go to the Sandwich Bay area to visit patients, but Grenfell said he'd already made the rounds there. Paddon asked how the people were and Grenfell replied that even the few husky dogs left there were staggering with hunger.

"I'm not surprised to hear that," said Paddon, "because when I was there in April, just before the breakup of the ice, even the people who were the best off were only eating dry bread and seal meat killed sometime during the winter. It was awful. To tell you the truth, I was expecting you to say there was no one left alive around the bay."

Grenfell lowered his head and wiped away tears, then whispered, "Would you leave me alone for a few moments, please. The scenes I saw as I went from house to house in Sandwich Bay in the last two days were too much for me. It's enough to break your heart." With that, he covered his face with his hands and cried.

Harry Paddon knew it was true. As he looked at Grenfell, he could picture every house and hut around Sandwich Bay and he felt anger well up against the fish merchants.

In a couple of minutes, Grenfell dried his eyes and apologized for being so "unprofessional."

"We might as well face it, Harry," he said. "Something has to be done. I mean we have to come up with some way to embarrass the people in Government House. It's obvious that nothing will move them, they just don't care."

"I know of a lot of things I'd like to see done, Wilfred," said Paddon.

"Name one. It might work."

Paddon looked up at the ceiling. "Let's start a campaign to move the people off the coast of Labrador," he said.

Grenfell thought for a few moments then quickly replied, "I've got an idea and I'll throw this at you." Looking around to make sure they were not being heard he asked Paddon to close the door and continued, "If every family now living around the Labrador Coast moved away it would be just what the fish merchants running the government want, to get rid of them." He paused. "But, you've got a great idea, and I think this is what we should do." He looked Paddon square in the eye. "How much nerve do you have for being a rebel, Harry?"

"You just try me," was Paddon's quick reply.

"Last fall, while I was traveling to the United States, I stopped off in Ottawa, Canada, for a meeting," said Grenfell. "While there I had the opportunity to meet the Premier of British Columbia, Mr. Richard McBride, a fine man." Grenfell paused. "In fact, he was in town to see me. He congratulated me on the work we are doing here in Labrador and offered me a proposal."

Grenfell looked out through the window at a schooner coming in the harbour and then continued. "He asked if I would be interested in coming to British Columbia to set up a Medical Mission like we have here. He guaranteed me his full support and said he would cooperate in every respect. I told him it was quite an offer and it would take some time to comment on such a request."

Paddon looked at him with a very surprised look.

"Don't worry, Harry, I'm not gone yet," said Grenfell. "About a month ago I had a letter from the Prime Minister of Canada, Mr. Robert Borden, and he made mention he had been talking to McBride about me going to British Columbia. He offered the Canadian government's full support if I decided to take on the challenge."

"What did you say?"

"I haven't answered yet," said Grenfell.

Paddon was silent.

"Can you see the picture?" asked Grenfell.

Paddon paused for a moment before looking at Grenfell and saying with excitement in his voice, "What an idea Wilfred, what an idea."

Grenfell knew then the young Englishman was prepared to go out on a limb for the people of Labrador.

"Before I write to Mr. Borden, I'm going to write our Prime Minister, Mr. Morris. It looks like there will be an election soon, and I'm going to tell him that we are considering moving to the West Coast of Canada unless steps are immediately taken to improve living conditions around the Labrador Coast and the Northern Peninsula. Our strongest move will be to outline some of the things we are sure would happen if a major outbreak of disease occurred during late fall or winter. We will also tell him about the terrible conditions people are experiencing and see what his reaction is, and decide from there what we will do."

"Do you think we should notify him as to what our intentions are?"

"No, not until we hear from him," said Grenfell. "In fact we'll send him a copy of the letter I had from the Canadian Prime Minister."

The two men huddled over the table.

"I know what we can do," said Paddon.

"What would you do?"

"I would make a proposal to the Prime Minister of Canada and ask him if he would be interested in financing the removal of, say, 200 families from Labrador to British Columbia."

"You certainly are a rebel," said Grenfell. "But I think we'll wait until we hear back from Morris and see if he's prepared to do anything for the people down here."

Dr. Harry Paddon was not a very patient man when it came to the Newfoundland government doing something for people on the Labrador, but he knew he would have to wait until his boss, Dr. Wilfred Grenfell, was ready.

"Okay, it's up to you," he said. The two physicians then left by boat to do a medical patrol further down on the Labrador Coast.

CHAPTER 10
Guns for Battle Harbour Co-op

In 1906, two years after graduating from Edinburgh University with a medical degree, Dr. John Grieve joined the Royal National Mission and began working for Dr. Grenfell in Battle Harbour, Labrador. From the first, there was no doubt he would leave his imprint along the Labrador Coast. He would tangle with the fish merchants who were plundering the Labrador people as well as summer fishermen from Newfoundland.

Before plunging into this story, however, it is important to know about some of the long term plans of the fish merchants, and I may point out that they were a very shrewd group of people. Let me take you back to Red Bay in 1896 when the first cooperative was formed and Dr. Grenfell had a run in with the business agent, Mr. Penney. The business he represented pulled out of Red Bay due to the co-op and Penney lost his job as an agent for the fish merchant. But this was not the end of Penney as the government, with the recommendation of the fish merchants, made him a magistrate for all of Labrador.

Penney said many times that Dr. Grenfell had destroyed his business and made him lose his job in Red Bay. He had said this to Dr. Grieve on at least one occasion, and so all of the Grenfell staff was fully aware of him and concerned he was out to do damage to Grenfell and his medical organization on the Labrador.

One day in the fall of 1911, Dr. Grieve was at St. Anthony on business. By now, he was well established at Battle Harbour and a shareholder in the cooperative there.

While in St. Anthony, he visited the community co-op in company with Grenfell. As they were walking through the store warehouse, Grieve noticed a stock of rifles.

Picking one up, he noticed they were Springfield rifles, old U.S. models corresponding to 45-70 Winchester.

"Great rifles," he said to Grenfell.

"Yes," said Grenfell. "When I was lecturing in the States, I met a gentleman who had a lot of these rifles in stock and he asked me if the people in the north could use them for hunting purposes. I assured him they could be of great use. He gave me 200 for the co-op, and as you can see there are about 50 left," he said.

Grieve asked if the Battle Harbour co-op could purchase those left, saying that Labrador men should have the opportunity to buy reasonably priced rifles for shooting caribou or seals. That fall, 20 of the rifles were sent to the Battle Harbour co-op. Grieve said later they were sold for $7 each to Labrador residents, a price that included enough ammunition to last them for a couple of years.

"It was the first rifles the men of Labrador had ever owned. The first thing they had to do was to learn how to shoot with them," Grieve said in telling his story.

It was said the fish merchants didn't want people in Labrador to have guns. It wasn't that the people were of a violent nature. It seemed the powerful fish merchants did not want these people becoming independent in any way, including with a hunting rifle.

CHAPTER 11
Run-in with Penney

In late afternoon of August 30, 1912, Dr. John Grieve was sitting at his desk in the office of the Battle Harbour hospital. He had been working for over 12 hours with a steady lineup of patients. Almost all the schooners that made up the massive Newfoundland fishing fleet were heading south after a successful voyage to Labrador. En-route, those with anyone ill aboard stopped off at Battle Harbour to see the doctor.

Dr. Grieve had a couple more patients to see for minor ailments before he could have a break from the long, busy day.

He was looking through a stack of papers and records of the day's work, trying to sort everything out, when a knock came on the office door.

He looked up, but before he could say 'come in' the door opened and a well-dressed man in his late forties stepped inside. "Good afternoon, Dr. Grieve," he said.

"Good afternoon," said the surprised doctor. "What can I do for you, sir?"

The man walked directly to the desk where Dr. Grieve sat and looked down at him. "I'm Magistrate Penney," he said.

Grieve held out his hand and stood up. "I was notified earlier today that you were coming to the coast," he said as they shook hands. Grieve sensed something was wrong.

"Dr. Grieve, may I sit down for a few moments?"

"Yes, of course," said Grieve, pointing to a chair and sitting down himself.

Penney tugged on the collar of his shirt and came right to the point, "Dr. Grieve, I'm not here on a social visit. I'm here, as you might say, on business." He didn't look at Grieve as he spoke, he was staring down at his hands.

Grieve was a master at judging character and sensed this as a weakness in Penney. He looked at the magistrate and got his attention.

"Magistrate Penney," he said. "I have had a very busy and long day and I still have two more patients to see, maybe we could have dinner later and discuss your business then."

"No," said Penney, looking Grieve in the eye. "We have dinner ready on our boat, but I'd like to ask you a couple of questions. I won't keep you very long."

"If it's only a couple of questions, then go ahead," said Grieve, sitting back in his chair.

Penney took a folded sheet of paper and a pencil from inside his coat pocket and placed it on the table.

"Dr. Grieve, are you the manager of the co-op here in Battle Harbour?"

Grieve paused for a moment then said, "No."

"Who is the manager, Doctor?"

"Isaac Cumby is the manager of the co-op."

"Are you sure?"

Dr. Grieve looked closer at Penney. He knew about the man, knew he was the former agent who'd run the mercantile business at Red Bay and been known as 'Captain Penney.'

He was the very man Dr. Grenfell had lectured the day the people formed the co-op at Red Bay years ago.

Grieve realized the man hated Grenfell and everything he stood for. He was also aware Penney was now in a position of authority. He was the King's representative on the Labrador.

He had the power to make or break anyone with just a wag of his tongue. Grieve didn't answer his last question. Penney then went right to the point.

"I'm investigating the sale of rifles to the people of Labrador and I want to know if you sold any to them?"

Grieve was not one who could be pushed around. He was afraid of nothing, not even the law, and everyone knew it.

"Listen, Penney," he said, dropping the title 'magistrate' and the respect that went with it. "I am astounded that you would barge into my office in the middle of a medical clinic and try to hold a court of law and have me convicted. You must be out of your mind. It's obvious to me you're here on some kind of a witch hunt trying to stir up trouble for the Mission. Or you have a personal grudge against Dr. Grenfell and you want to drag me into the trap you're trying to set."

"I am not setting a trap for anyone, Doctor," said Penney, getting mad and pointing his finger at Grieve. "Let me remind you that you will address me as magistrate because I am the authority here in Labrador."

"Listen, Magistrate…instead of being a magistrate trying to disrupt this mission, you should be a volunteer for Dr. Grenfell, following him around the world, helping to raise funds to build new hospitals and an orphanage here on the Labrador. You should be helping him raise funds to start new cooperative stores around the Labrador Coast instead of trying to destroy the ones that are already established and working fine."

Penney stood up. He was furious as he struck the table with each word he spoke, "Grenfell put me out of business a few years ago at Red Bay and I haven't forgotten it."

Grieve knew he had Penney where he wanted him. By now he was so mad he could hardly speak.

"I'm going to ask you a question, Magistrate. Did the fish merchants send you here on a mission of hate? Is this the beginning of a campaign to drive Dr. Grenfell off the Labrador Coast?" Grieve stood up and faced the strong arm of the law. "Are you here carrying out the wishes of the fish merchants, or are you upset because people along the Labrador Coast have had a little better way of life for a few years?"

Penney knew it was no use arguing with this stubborn doctor. He turned quickly and headed for the door.

"Just a minute, Magistrate, before you leave," said Grieve. Penney turned around and looked at him. "I think we should get together later and continue our debate."

Penney turned quickly and stamped out the door.

At 9.30 that night a summons was served on Dr. John Grieve at his home, ordering him to appear in court at Battle Harbour at noon the next day, August 30.

Sergeant Alexander Dwyer of the Newfoundland Constabulary served the summons which stated that Grieve was charged under the Customs Act, Section 96, sub section 115, for failing to pay Customs duty on rifles sold to people in Labrador.

Dwyer, a St. John's man, was assigned to patrol the Labrador Coast during the summer months. On this particular trip he was accompanying Magistrate Penney along the coast, holding court whenever possible.

A few years earlier, Dwyer himself had a run-in with the Mission. Alex, as everyone called him, had eight children back home in St. John's. In those days policemen were paid a very low salary. So low in fact that the police sergeant and his family lived far below the poverty line and had to scrounge everything they could to survive.

On a particular patrol, Dwyer was in St. Anthony on his way back to St. John's. When he arrived at St. Anthony he went to see Noah Simms, Customs Officer for the area. While he was there, Simms told him about clothes that had come in from the United States and Canada with no duty paid, and no duty due to be paid.

"The clothes are given to the poor in exchange for things such as firewood, salt fish, knitted goods or vegetables, or anything else that can be used on the Mission," he said.

Hearing that, Dwyer indicated he would like to have some of the clothes for his family.

"I don't have anything to exchange but I am among the poor and that's for sure," he said.

"I know how you can get some of that stuff," said Simms.

"How?" Dwyer asked quickly.

"You must know someone here in St. Anthony who has a vegetable garden and owes you a favour?"

"Yes, I certainly do," said Dwyer after a moment's thought.

"Well then, go and get some vegetables from them and take them to the Mission and exchange them for clothes."

Dwyer did exactly that and came back to Simms' office with a large sack full of children's clothes. He then headed for home on the steamer.

Shortly afterwards, a Mission official found out about what had happened. He took the matter to his superior and it was suspected Dwyer was trying to set them up and get them in trouble for breaking the Customs rules. They thought this was something the fish merchants could use against them.

The official went to the head superintendent of the Mission who telegraphed a report of the incident to the police chief at St. John's.

The police were waiting for Dwyer when he arrived. After they questioned him, he admitted having the children's clothes. The bag of clothes was seized and he never saw it again, but no disciplinary action was taken against him. After that incident, though, he had no liking for Grenfell or his Mission. He always said they had tried to get him in trouble.

And now here he was in Battle Harbour sitting down with Magistrate Penney putting together a summons for Dr. Grieve of the Mission under the Customs Act. It made him feel good.

The third man sitting at the table that night was Josiah Gosse, Customs Officer and Welfare Officer for all of Labrador for the period June 1 to October 30.

The three men sat at a table aboard the patrol boat and put together the case they thought would cause a mortal blow to Grenfell's Mission on the Labrador Coast.

Josiah Gosse sat across the small table from Magistrate Penney. He seemed excited.

Penney was still mad about the lecture he'd received from Dr. Grieve.

"Listen, Joseph," said Gosse. "We've got them cold. Isaac Cumby told me this morning he bought one of these rifles and fifty rounds of ammunition from Dr. Grieve last fall. And Frank Lewis, the winter caretaker for Baine Johnston, said he knew for sure Dr. Grieve had the guns come over from St. Anthony and he sold them without any duty being paid on them. What we should do is summon the two of them to court for tomorrow as witnesses against Grieve."

"Okay, okay," said a still upset Penney. "Go to work and write up the summons for the two of them to appear in court as witnesses against Grieve for tomorrow."

"Do you think I should go and have a talk to Dr. Grieve," asked Dwyer.

"I just came from the office of that Scotsman. He was born ignorant and I guess he will stay ignorant till he dies," said Penney as he threw up his hands. "There's no need to go see him, it's time wasted. Write out the summons and serve it on Grieve tonight. I don't care if it's at midnight. Just make sure he's in court at noon tomorrow."

Dr. Grieve was not a very pleasant man when he walked into the little Grenfell schoolhouse at noon on August 31, 1912. It was Saturday and supposed to be his day off after a very busy week. When he came through the door the three men seated at the table looked at him and sensed his anger. Grieve was accompanied by his secretary, who was carrying a typewriter. They both sat down.

CHAPTER 12

Grieve in Court

S ergeant Dwyer stood up. "All rise," he said. "His Majesty's court is now in session. I declare this court open in the name of His Majesty the King, Judge Penney presiding. God save the King. Please be seated."

Penney picked up a sheet of paper and read the name on it. "Mr. John Grieve," he said loud and clear.

"I am present," said Grieve.

A chair was placed in front of the magistrate.

"Would you sit in this chair, Dr. Grieve?"

Grieve sat and Penney looked straight in his eyes as he asked, "Are you Dr. John Grieve?"

"Yes, Your Honour," said Grieve.

"Did you receive a summons last night to appear here in court at noon today, Dr. Grieve?" asked Penney.

"No," said Grieve.

Penney's eyes widened in surprise, he looked at Gosse and Dwyer with disbelief.

The two officers looked at Grieve, then back at Penney, but said nothing. Penney managed to keep his cool as he turned to Dwyer and asked, "Did you serve a summons on Dr. Grieve last night, to appear here in this court today at twelve noon?"

"Yes, Your Honour, I served it to him personally at 9 p.m. at his home and he signed it. You have the copy he signed in front of you."

"Well, Dr. Grieve, what have you to say to that?" asked Penney. "Are you trying to pull a fast one on this court? Because if you are, I will have you arrested and jailed."

"No, Your Honour," said Grieve. "If you will give me a moment please, I'll explain."

He asked his secretary to hand him the court file and when she did he took out the summons Dwyer had issued to him. He handed the summons to Penney and asked, "Is this paper like the carbon copy you have in front of you, Your Honour?"

Penney took the paper and looked it over carefully. "Yes, it's exactly the same as the one I have here."

"Well then, Your Honour, if the two are alike then I wasn't summoned to appear in court today. On that summons, it says I have to appear before you at 12 noon on August 30. This happens to be August 31, Your Honour."

Penney's eyes scanned the paper again and sure enough it was true. "Sergeant Dwyer," he said, "how could you be so stupid to serve a summons like this?"

"It wasn't me, Your Honour. I never wrote it out. It was Gosse that wrote up the summons. I only served it."

Before Penney had a chance to tear a strip off Gosse, Grieve spoke up. "It's not Mr. Gosse, Your Honour. It's you, Magistrate Penney, you're the one who signed it before it was served on me. Surely you read it before you signed it?"

Penney was embarrassed but furious. He thought for a moment then said brusquely, "You're here anyway, so let's get on with the case."

"It's not as simple as that, Your Honour," said Grieve. "We're in the King's Court now and there are guidelines and procedures that must be followed. I happen to know because I am a justice of the peace and have studied many aspects of the law, especially court procedures."

Penney was speechless. He realized he had been too hasty in trying to get something on Grieve that would embarrass Grenfell and make him important in the eyes of the fish merchants of St. John's. There was a silence in the court for a couple of minutes, then Dr. Grieve spoke, "Magistrate Penney, I am very anxious to get on with this case and find what the charge is that you have against me, therefore all you have to do is amend the date from the 30th to the 31st and proceed with the case."

Penney cleared his throat. "I am changing the date in question from the 30th to the 31st and we will proceed with the case. Are you ready to precede, Dr. Grieve?" he asked.

Grieve couldn't believe Penney was holding court this way. He thought about the poor souls along the coast of Labrador who didn't know the difference and wondered what kind of injustice they must be getting from this man.

"No," he said, adding, "Your Honour."

Penney looked at Grieve and said, "We are going to proceed with this case, Dr. Grieve, and we're going to proceed now."

Well," said Grieve, "if that's the case I am going to plead not guilty as charged."

"Very good," said Penney, turning to Dwyer. "Bring in your first witness, Sergeant."

"Yes, Your Honour," said Dwyer.

"Your Honour, may I have a minute to ask Mr. Gosse a question or two before you bring in your first witness?" asked Grieve.

Penney held up his hand. "Just a moment, Sergeant," he said to Dwyer. "We will let Dr. Grieve ask Mr. Gosse a couple of questions before we proceed."

"Thank you sir, " said Grieve as he looked at Gosse. "There's no doubt you can bring many witnesses into this court who bought rifles from the co-op last fall. However the charge here is not the sale of rifles and ammunition to local people. The charge here says that the co-op did not pay duty on rifles that were sold at Battle Harbour, Labrador, contrary to Section 96, subsection 115 of the Customs Act. Is this correct, Mr. Gosse?"

Gosse looked at Penney then at Grieve. "Yes that's right, that is what the charge says," he said.

"Then my question to you is this, Mr. Gosse, do you have any proof to present to this court today that the duty was not paid on these rifles, either in the form of a certified letter or a telegram from Mr. Simms, the Customs Officer at St. Anthony which was the rifles' point of entry? Or do you have such a letter or telegram from the head Customs office at St. John's stating the duty wasn't paid. The witness you are about to bring in doesn't know anything about whether or not the duty was paid, therefore his evidence will be a waste of time."

"No sir, I don't," said Gosse. "But before I left St. John's I heard my boss say that as far as he was concerned there was no duty paid on them rifles that were sold down here last year, and I believe him."

"Mr. Gosse, let me tell you something. I know your boss, he's a fine gentleman. However, people make mistakes and sometime people misunderstand each other. But I want to let you know that my boss, Dr. Grenfell, is a gentleman too and I believe him. He says that the Customs duty was paid on these rifles at the point of entry in St. Anthony."

Gosse didn't know what to say.

Grieve turned to Penney and said, "The strong point is this, if Mr. Gosse has charged me and made me stand in His Majesty's court without having substantial proof that a breach of the law has been committed then he is breaking the law himself."

Penney was dumfounded. He looked at Gosse to see if he had an answer but none came. Josiah Gosse was stopped dead in his tracks.

Grieve saw his chance to have his say.

"The law is for you and for me, Mr. Gosse. I am a physician and there are laws governing everything I do. You are no different. In this instance, it appears you are pressing ahead with a case against me and the Mission without having any real facts on paper or any sworn evidence. For that reason, I am asking for a postponement."

"Not on your life," said Gosse.

"Mr. Gosse," said Grieve. "This is not your court. This happens to be His Majesty's court with Magistrate Penney presiding. If the Minister of Justice knew you were here in Labrador controlling the court, you would be in serious trouble."

"Order in the court," Penney said loudly. "There will be no postponement of this case, Dr. Grieve. Get on with it, Sergeant Dwyer."

"Magistrate Penney," said Grieve in a bold voice. "We have to face facts and look at what is happening here, and I should remind the court that everything said has been recorded by my stenographer." Everyone looked at the woman with the typewriter. "Can you imagine if a copy of these court proceedings appeared in the Associated Press in New York? What would the world think of our justice system? Imagine someone reading that a loyal citizen had asked for a postponement but the judge refused because he wanted to get a conviction regardless of the evidence."

Penney was furious. He hammered the table in front of him with his fist as he looked at Gosse and Dwyer and then almost screamed. "I am calling a recess for five minutes."

"All rise," said Dwyer.

He asked for everyone to leave the one-room school and wait outside. As they were leaving, Grieve whispered to the secretary, telling her to take her files and the typewriter outside with her.

Magistrate Penney did not like what he saw but said nothing. When the court resumed, he stood up and said, "Dr. Grieve, I am granting you a postponement, you may go."

"Thank you, Your Honour," said Grieve.

As he turned to leave, he looked at the three men who were staring at him with hate in their eyes. It was then he realized this was the beginning of trouble for Dr. Grenfell, for the Mission in Labrador, and for him.

The troubles Dr. Grenfell had with his Medical Mission in Northern Newfoundland and Labrador stemmed from the government of the day and were engineered by the fish merchants. There was no doubt about it. They were out to get him.

CHAPTER 13

Arch in St. John's

When the fisheries patrol vessel *Petrel* arrived at the dock in St. John's it was met by a government car. Archibald Piccott stepped onto the wharf. He was a bit stiff-legged after his long journey from Battle Harbour. The weather had been rough for the last twenty-four hours. The man driving the car knew him well and shook hands with him. After he got aboard the car the driver noticed the claw marks on his face.

"What happened to you, Arch?" he asked.

"That's a long story," said Piccott. "I got attacked by a she-bear in Battle Harbour."

His driver looked puzzled but was anxious to hear the rest of the story, not now but later. He was sure that the she-bear was not an animal.

After Piccott left Battle Harbour aboard the *Petrel*, he had plenty of time to think and plan what he would do to cause trouble for Grenfell and the Grenfell Mission when he got back to St. John's. Most of the members of the House of Assembly were fish merchants, or involved with the fishing industry. Most of them had business strung out along the Labrador Coast and around the Northern Newfoundland coast where Grenfell operated. As far as Piccott was concerned, all the merchants were suffering.

"If Grenfell is allowed to continue the way he's going there won't be a business owned by the fish merchants left along the Labrador Coast within ten years. The cooperatives will control it all," Piccott said to Captain Kennedy. "This Grenfell has to be stopped and I've got a plan."

Kennedy wasn't overly concerned about what Piccott had in mind. The only thing he knew was that there was a big improvement in the living conditions down north since Grenfell had arrived 15 years ago. However, this was none of his concern so he kept quiet.

Piccott knew there wasn't much sense in talking about the matter anymore. For years there had been talk but no one had the nerve to plan something. Now the time was ripe to make a move.

The government car took Piccott directly to his office at the Colonial Building. He wanted to meet with his colleagues looking the same as when he was attacked at Battle Harbour. The dried blood was still on his face.

On his way into the Colonial Building he met an old friend and one time colleague, Walter Baine Grieve.

Walter was the owner of the fishing business at Battle Harbour. Although they shared the same surname, he wasn't a relative of Dr. John Grieve and had no use for him.

After Magistrate Penney got Grieve in court for evasion of Customs duty, Walter did everything he could to try and get Grieve and his wife kicked out of Battle Harbour but was unsuccessful. From then on, Walter became an enemy of the Grenfell organization.

Seeing Piccott, Walter stood and stared. "What in the good heavens happened to you, Arch, strike an iceberg?" he asked.

"Come in the office, I've got something to tell you," said Piccott.

Walter followed him in and closed the door.

"I got attacked by a woman over a bucket of bakeapples on the beach in Battle Harbour," said Piccott, holding up his hand when he saw Walter put his head down and laugh. "Hold on a minute till I tell you what went on then you won't laugh," he said and went on to tell the whole story.

When he'd finished telling what the root of the whole problem was, Walter said, "You always told me I was a liar when I used to tell you about what the Grenfell bunch were doing down on the Labrador Coast. You laughed when Penney came back with his tail between his legs after having Dr. Grieve in court, and here you are now with your face half hanging off. I've got no pity for you. You won't do anything about this either because you're afraid."

Walter knew the Minister of Fisheries and Marine Services was mad. He could tell by the expression on Piccott's face that he was determined not to let this incident go by.

"Now you listen to me Walter," said Piccott. "Enough is enough. I'm going directly to the Prime Minister with a complaint about what's going on with the Grenfell Mission down on the Labrador Coast...I can't believe it. I've come back wounded from Labrador. We never thought it was as serious as this, Walter. Wherever we went, we met people who hated the government and the fish merchants and even had the nerve to tell you that point blank. It almost sounds like a revolution to me."

Walter never thought he would see the day when he could tackle the cooperative movement down on the Labrador, but now he knew something would be done.

"Listen Arch," he said, "when will you be able to attend a meeting and get something on paper concerning this whole matter, because it's long overdue?"

In the two years since the Penney/Grieve court case, Walter had been after Piccott and the rest of the members of the House of Assembly involved with the fishing industry to investigate what was going on with the Grenfell Mission down on the Labrador and around Northern Newfoundland and stop all those cooperatives from being formed.

Why, Grenfell was having all of the dry goods and clothing donated to the poor people of Labrador come into the country duty free and selling them below the merchant's prices, putting them all out of business and even closing up shops!

"Listen Walter," said Piccott. "I am going to the Prime Minister right now and let him see what kind of state I'm in."

"I think that's a good idea," said Walter. He knew Prime Minister Edward Morris would have to get riled up before anything was done, and right now with Arch Piccott on the war path he knew this was a good time to put the fish merchants plan in place. Walter also knew that he would never be able to get into Morris's office because the Prime Minister hated him, but Piccott could deliver the message for him.

"Arch, while you are in Morris's office, I want you to deliver a message to him from the fish merchants. Make sure, though, you don't mention my name or tell him you were talking to me."

Walter knew the plan he and his fish merchant buddies had cooked up would cause panic for the Prime Minister because Morris was very concerned about finances. No matter what else happened, Morris knew the fish merchants were the backbone of the financial structure of the Colony and had to be treated with respect.

Walter cleared his throat and said, "Tell him that the fish merchants along the Labrador Coast are not going down there next year unless the government steps in and puts a stop to Grenfell and his gang. And tell him if that happens, Newfoundland will go broke overnight."

Piccott couldn't believe what he was hearing. "What a plan," he said. "This will drive the old man out of his mind."

"That's our plan Arch, come hell or high water."

Piccott said nothing else. Hurriedly getting up from his chair he headed for the office of the Prime Minister.

CHAPTER 14
Starving in Labrador

During the winter of 1911, people along the Labrador Coast came close to starving. In testimony given under oath by Dr. John Grieve during the enquiry it was revealed that insufficient food was brought to Labrador for the winter season and this created a terrible crisis. It was suspected the fish merchants engineered everything because of the cooperatives.

By the end of February, people along the coast of Labrador and Northern Newfoundland were living on whatever they could get off the land or along the beaches. At the end of March when the ice began to melt, people started collecting mussels along the shoreline to try and feed their families. The saying was, "the people were scraping the beaches to find a living." Beriberi, a disease of the peripheral nerves resulting from the absence of B vitamins in the diet, was beginning to set in. In April, according to Dr. Grieve, the people were living on mussels.

On April 29, the following telegram was sent to the Government of Newfoundland:

April 29, 1911.
To the Colonial Secretary of the
Government of Newfoundland
Sir:
People from Battle Harbour to Cartwright will starve
unless flour comes soon.
No flour at Battle Harbour or Cartwright.
Can you send Steamer north?
Send twenty barrels of flour by HOME!
Signed Dr. John Grieve. J. P. (Justice of the Peace).

Another telegram was sent to Dr. Grenfell, who was at his New York office, informing him of the deplorable state of affairs at Battle Harbour and Cartwright and along the Labrador Coast. Grieve also told Grenfell he had wired St. John's that people were starving and requested a meeting with him in St. John's.

When the telegram marked "private" arrived at Dr. Grenfell's office in New York, it was opened by a secretary who read it and handed it over to a representative of the Associated Press who was in the office at the time, which she had no right to do.

The reporter took a copy. He then went straight to his newspaper office with the story and published it.

The next day under the dateline St. John's, Newfoundland, the headline screamed: PEOPLE ARE PAUPERS, DYING OF STARVATION ON THE LABRADOR.

The story described conditions on the Labrador Coast and gave the Newfoundland government a black eye. This created an awful commotion when the news reached St. John's. The fish merchants in the government were not going to stand for it. The newspaper article was also embarrassing for Dr. Grenfell and Dr. John Grieve because no one had starved to death as of that date. Grieve and Grenfell had to explain what had happened.

About a week after Dr. Grieve sent the telegram to St. John's, people started coming down with scurvy, a disease caused by lack of Vitamin C in the diet and characterized by swollen and bleeding gums and great weakness.

The Anglican clergyman at Battle Harbour, the Reverend T. Gardiner, asked Dr. Grieve if he would get a crew of men together and launch one of the merchant's small schooners and go to ports further south in search of food. This was impossible due to heavy ice, and Grieve knew too that if it had been done civil suits would never end for him and anyone else involved.

When Walter Baine Grieve heard about the starvation conditions, he contacted Magistrate Penney and had him wire Dr. Grieve, who was the justice of the peace, telling him to organize something to protect his Battle Harbour property from people breaking in and stealing food. Grieve refused. This created quite a fuss for him down the road.

When copies of the Associated Press story reached St. John's, the Prime Minister had a lot of questions to answer. He told reporters he was immediately sending a ship loaded with supplies to the Labrador Coast.

Two days later, on May 2, supplies were on board the mail ship *Prospero* on the way to Labrador.

On May 15, the ship reached Fox Harbour on the Labrador Coast and the desperate situation was relieved.

It is certain that if the telegram had not been published in the newspapers of New York the *Prospero* would never have been sent to Labrador.

CHAPTER 15

Walter Baine Grieve

Walter Baine Grieve came from a family involved in business in Newfoundland and Scotland. His father was a well-known merchant and member of the Executive Council of the Government, appointed by the Governor of Newfoundland. At an early age, Walter took over the family business in Newfoundland and expanded into the fishing industry. He owned large vessels which carried goods and fish products to many countries around the world.

In 1909, he found himself involved in a campaign against Sir Edward Morris, leader of the People's Party. Things got nasty when rumors became rampant that Walter was a secret supporter of a scheme to have Newfoundland become a province of Canada. This resulted in charges being laid against him. Morris had him arrested April 22, 1909, but he was never brought to trial.

During World War I, Walter played a very active part in promoting the war effort throughout Newfoundland. But, above everything, he was a very clever businessman who built one of the largest fishing enterprises in Newfoundland. Right now, though, he was a very angry man, bent on revenge against Grenfell and his Medical Mission for organizing cooperative stores among the fishermen along the Labrador Coast. Worst of all was that Grenfell had dared start a co-op store right under his nose at Battle Harbour, where Walter had set him up with his first hospital in 1892. That was unforgivable as far as Walter was concerned.

Walter also couldn't understand why a physician wanted to educate people about their finances. "It's not the business of doctors to tell fishermen how much they should get paid for their catch, it's none of their business anyway, that's our concern," he would say whenever he talked to anyone.

And now, as he walked along the sidewalk in the centre of old St. John's, Walter felt a little peace of mind for the first time since the cooperative racket at Battle Harbour started.

He knew what had to be done.

First was to get the Prime Minister riled up and scared.

"We will have the government carry out a full investigation of everything going on and get Grenfell booted out of Labrador," he whispered out loud, feeling good.

He wondered who would have the nerve to tackle such a job and immediately came up with a name.

"We will have Magistrate Penney head the enquiry. He's the one that Grenfell kicked out of Red Bay years ago. Yes sir, that's just who we'll get to do the job, Magistrate Penney." Walter stopped and laughed aloud. "Imagine the headlines. Penney gets kicked out of Red Bay by Grenfell, then Penney kicks Grenfell out of Labrador." With that thought in mind he laughed again and walked on.

The Honourable Archibald Piccott had no trouble getting in to see the Prime Minister. All he did was open the door and walk in. Sir Edward Morris was surprised to see him, especially with a scratched, bloody face.

"It looks to me like the Minister of Marine and Fisheries ran into some kind of trouble down on the Labrador," he said, looking over his reading glasses.

"Some kind of trouble?" said Piccott, as he shut the door. "I was lucky to escape with my life."

"Tell me what happened," Morris said with concern in his voice.

Piccott outlined what had happened to him at Battle Harbour, making every detail ten times as bad as it really was.

"I was lucky to escape without having serious injuries, Edward. To tell you the truth, I suppose it's lucky I only had one hand because if I had two hands I may have choked her."

Piccott went on to tell what he had been told and had seen for himself about the co-ops on the Labrador Coast.

"If something is not done about this very soon I can see a total collapse of the cod fishery on the Labrador," he told Morris.

"Why would you say that, Arch? How can that happen?"

"Every fish merchant on the Labrador is saying that unless the government steps in and takes control and shuts down all of the co-ops along the Labrador, they are going to boycott the fishery next year. And if this happens, you know better then I do what will happen to the Colony."

Morris was silent. He had not been expecting to hear this statement from his fisheries minister.

"This is a very serious statement you are making, Arch. Are you serious about what you're saying?"

"At every merchant place I visited along the Labrador Coast and the Northern Peninsula, the owners or their representatives told me the same thing. They are all fed up with those co-ops."

Morris stood up and walked around his office. He stopped and looked out the window. He had been hearing complaints for the last few years about this problem, but never anything like this. This was serious.

Piccott again spoke up. "Do you know what would happen if the fish merchants boycotted the Labrador fishery for one season, Edward? The Bank could crash, and if that happened, the Colony could fall flat on her face."

Morris knew this was true because the Labrador fishery was the backbone of the Newfoundland economy. To stop it for one year would deal a mortal blow to the import-export business the Colony relied on.

Morris turned to Piccott and said, "You're the Fisheries Minister, so why don't you do something about it?"

"What do you want me to do about it?"

"I don't care what you do. Just do something that will prevent this from happening."

"I'll do my best, but it's a big job to tackle," said Piccott as he left Morris's office.

As he walked down the hallway, he was laughing inside, sure that his best would cause a mortal blow to Grenfell and his cooperatives on the Labrador.

After Piccott cleaned himself up, he immediately went to Walter Grieve's office on Water Street. The girl at the front desk recognized him and ushered him into her boss's office.

Walter was not surprised to see him.

"I bet the old man almost jumped out of his skin when you told him what I told you, Arch."

"Almost jumped out of his skin is not the word," said Piccott. "He almost jumped out of the window."

Walter laughed. "What did he say?"

"He told me to get to work on it immediately and get something done about it."

Walter was excited. He knew this was his chance to get even with Grenfell and stamp out the cooperative movement on the Labrador Coast.

"Make sure you write down the date, time and what he told you. Because all of this will become important down the road when things start to move," he said.

Piccott agreed that this would be done.

Walter rang a bell and when the girl came in he ordered coffee and something to eat. "A snack for both of us, please," he said. When the girl left, he turned to Arch. "You know what has to be done don't you?" he said.

Piccott waited for Walter to continue.

"We have to get our lawyers working on this for us. They will have to put together a petition and present it to the House of Assembly along with the signature of every fish merchant now operating on the Labrador Coast."

"What a great idea that is, Walter, yes sir. That is certainly one of the thing we will have to do."

The girl arrived with the coffee and two sandwiches.

"Do you think we will have any trouble getting the rest of the fish merchants to sign the petitions?" Piccott asked after she left.

"Trouble?" said Walter. "The only trouble we'll have is trying to stop them from signing before the petition is completed."

The two men talked for an hour about what they would do and the wording that should go on the petition.

"Have you got a list of all the merchants who operated down there this summer, Arch?"

"To my knowledge, there were about twenty down there this summer that were of any size," said Piccott.

Walter knew them all personally. However, he was aware that only about a dozen of the merchants had any commercial impact on the fishing industry along the Labrador Coast.

"If we can get a dozen firms to sign the petition we will have about 80 per cent of the total fishing business that's done down there. As for the wording of the petition and getting everything drawn up, you can leave that to me. But you will have to help when it comes to getting it into the hands of the elected members and the Prime Minister."

"That won't be a problem because most of the members in the House are shareholders in the fishing companies down on the Labrador and they're the ones doing most of the screaming," said Piccott.

"Don't worry. I'll have the signatures on the petition," said Walter.

"I'll depend on that," said Piccott.

After they exchanged a few more words, Walter assured Piccott he would keep him up to date on whatever happened.

"My office is open to you at all times, just come in anytime," he told his close friend.

CHAPTER 16

The Petition

W alter knew what had to be done as far as getting a
petition before the government legislators. He had
money, friends, and the ability to get things done.

He first called the company lawyers, briefed them on what he
was planning to do, and got their advice.

The lawyers told him what he was up against and noted Dr.
Grenfell had a lot of influence with the Prime Minister and the
Governor, Mr. Macgregor.

They also told him that the leader of the Opposition, Mr.
William Lloyd, would not be in favour of a scheme against
Grenfell's Mission because Lloyd, like Grenfell, was an
Englishman.

"Lloyd will give us a lot of trouble," said the lawyers.

"I can control Lloyd," said Walter. "He's the least of our
worries because he's jumping around all over the place, from Party
to Party."

(Journalist Michael Harrington characterized Lloyd as a
scrupulous person and a scholarly man who was just a babe in the
woods in the jungle of Newfoundland politics.)

After a long debate, the lawyers were convinced. They put
together a petition to take to the House of Assembly, or rather to
first put in front of the fish merchants for their signatures, and then
to the House of Assembly, where they would have the Honourable
Archibald Piccott introduce it.

It took about a month for Walter and his lawyers to put
together the terms of the petition and prepare a draft copy for the
fish merchants to view.

Walter was careful in contacting the Labrador fish merchants. He knew some of them didn't care what the Grenfell crowd did, as long as there was somewhere to get a tooth pulled or something taken out of your eye. He knew who they were and had no intention of asking them to come to his office and look at the petition.

Including Walter's, there were eight large firms long the Labrador Coast that bought approximately 85 per cent of all the fish products produced there.

He had talked to these merchants on many occasions and they were all in a rage with the cooperative movement and demanding something be done.

Within a week or so, Walter had spoken to all the merchants, telling them what he was doing and setting a date for their first meeting.

He said Fisheries Minister Piccott would be attending the meeting. He told them what had happened to Arch on his trip to the Labrador a few weeks before. It became a big joke in their circle, and Walter made sure that keeping Piccott mad was their biggest asset.

In about three weeks, one of the lawyers, a Mr. Wood, came to Walter's office, carrying the newly drafted petition for him to look at. The following is the actual wording of the draft that he presented to Walter:

TO THE HONOURABLE HOUSE OF ASSEMBLY

The Petition of the undersigned Humbly Sheweth:

1. *That your petitioners are engaged in the mercantile business of the colony and have large undertakings on the Coast of Labrador.*
2. *That Competition is very keen where so many rival interests are involved.*
3. *That for many years your petitioners have silently acquiesced in the competition of charitable organizations*

in the interest of the poorer class of fishermen who have derived benefits there from.

4. *That on misrepresentations that this dependency of Newfoundland is largely composed of paupers, the charity of the generous people of the United States has been greatly stimulated and the benefits in money and have been so largely increased that they have now become a menace to all other mercantile concerns on that coast who have to pay duty and freight upon the material they use or vend in the prosecution of the fisheries there.*

5. *That the privileges heretofore extended to the International Grenfell Association of America, successors to the Royal Mission to Deep Sea Fishermen should either be sensibly curtailed or abolished not only on account of the above reasons but seeing that it is affiliated to certain stores trading on the coast and thereby they have an outlet for the sale of duty free merchandise introduced under the caption of goods for charitable purposes.*

6. *That your petitioners have reason to believe that these stores are capitalized by American Philanthropists who have invested without any idea of receiving dividend or interest.*

7. *That this is no mere assumption as evidence exists that the Customs Authorities have detected breaches of the Law and have compelled payment to be made by the Association.*

Your petitioners therefore humbly pray that your Honourable House will cause enquiry to be made as to the correctness of these allegations with a view to their removal or remedy.

And as in duty bound your petitioners will humbly pray.

St. John's, NF.

Walter read the petition a couple of times and was quite satisfied with the wording. He gave orders to his lawyers to contact the merchants involved with the petition and arrange a meeting at his office at 2 p.m. the following day.

Shortly before the meeting started, he showed them a copy of the petition. After everyone had a chance to review the wording, it was agreed it would be open for a discussion, piece by piece, to see if any changes needed to be made. Walter made sure no copy of the petition left the meeting.

One merchant wanted a section added demanding the immediate removal of Dr. John Grieve from the Labrador Coast, calling him a murderer.

"We have to be careful what we say about individuals personally for fear of a civil case against us," cautioned lawyer Wood.

The gentleman, however, was very upset and said he could prove that Dr. Grieve intentionally turned away a young child belonging to a Mr. Emerson of Carbonear who was down fishing at Mattie's Cove, Labrador. The merchant said that Grieve drove Emerson and his three-year-old daughter from the hospital because she had measles and refused to admit or treat her. He said Emerson took the little girl back to his shack and she died two days later.

"If that's not murder then what is it?" said the man, adding, "I know this to be true because the man told me about it himself after he came back."

"This is the kind of thing that has to be brought out but not in the petition," said Walter. "You can talk about it when you are called to testify during the enquiry. You'll get your chance in front of the newspaper reporters. That's why we need an enquiry, to get it out in the open. If we can get the government to conduct an enquiry we will demand that Emerson be interviewed in front of the commissioner. Hopefully, it will be Magistrate Penney."

During their four hour meeting, they agreed that the group would recommend Penney as commissioner, would, in fact, demand him because they were sure that he could do the job on Grenfell.

It was also agreed they would pressure the Prime Minister with the threat of boycotting the Labrador fishery if something wasn't done about the situation immediately.

Lawyer Wood warned them this would be a very tricky piece of business because Dr. Grenfell was a very popular man with the Governor and the international community, especially in the United States and Canada.

"The people along the Labrador Coast think he's God, therefore they may not stand for too much pressure from the government and especially from the fish merchants, so you have to tread very carefully," said Wood. "The Prime Minister may be afraid of a backlash from the international community."

"We know how far we can go," said Walter.

Wood said no more.

Before they adjourned, it was agreed they would meet again in December after everything was clued up from the year's business activity.

CHAPTER 17
Questions

D uring this time, World War I was raging in Europe and affecting the whole world. Thousands of Newfoundlanders were dying on the battlefields of Europe. The problem with the cooperatives and the fish merchants along the Labrador Coast seemed trivial when compared to a war that was touching so many.

But the merchants convinced government officials that something had to be done about the co-op racket, war or no war, or else the whole fishing business along the Labrador Coast would be ruined and the economy of Newfoundland would collapse.

The government of the day, which was controlled by the fish merchants, determined to push through some kind of solution. Archibald Piccott told his colleagues that come hell or high water Grenfell, Grieve and Paddon were not going to get away with it. They had to go.

It has been proven over and over again that to keep any kind of a secret is literally impossible. That applied to the fish merchants' committee headed by Walter Baine Grieve. Members of the committee vowed they would not tell anyone about what went on during their meetings, but this was not the case. Some members leaked the fact they were going to suggest to the government that Magistrate Penney should head the enquiry.

By the time the news reached the Grenfell Mission down north, and the people along the Labrador Coast, rumour had it that Penney had already been given the job. This caused quite a stir among the Grenfell staff, especially at Battle Harbour.

Truth was, though, that no decision had yet been made on a commissioner.

During the late fall of 1916, Dr. Grenfell made a trip down north along the Labrador. When he got to Battle Harbour, he picked up Dr. John Grieve and they worked their way further north, attending to the sick and needy and holding clinics in every nook and cranny. There was a cold chilly wind blowing with a dusting of snow when they arrived at the North West River Hospital in the late November afternoon. They found Dr. Paddon a very busy man as the population of North West River was beginning to swell due to the return of those who had been out on the coast fishing for the summer.

Everyone was expecting Dr. Grenfell and this made for a lot of activity. The wharf where his medical boat landed was crowded with people. After all the excitement had died down, the three doctors went to the hospital and spent several hours discussing medical and administrative business before retiring to the dining room.

It was obvious to Paddon that Grenfell and Grieve had some other important business they wanted to discuss.

Before they sat down for a meal of fresh pork from the Mission butcher shop at North West River, accompanied by vegetables grown in the Mission garden, Grenfell asked Paddon if he had heard anything new regarding the fish merchants request for a government enquiry into wrongdoing between the co-op stores and the Mission.

Paddon said he hadn't received any mail since September, "not even a newspaper." He asked, "Have you heard anything new?"

Grieve was the first to reply. "Yes, we heard that the fish merchants have made a request to the House of Assembly for a commissioner to head the enquiry."

"That's very good," said Paddon.

During dinner, they continued to discuss the government enquiry.

"Does the government have anyone in mind as commissioner?" asked Paddon.

"Yes, I think they have. In fact, we heard through the grapevine they have selected someone," said Grieve.

"And who would that be?" asked Paddon.

Grieve ignored the question as he looked at the well-prepared plate of dinner in front of him. "This looks delicious," he said.

Paddon thanked him and replied, "I'll pass your remarks along to my wife, the cook."

"We'll thank her personally a little later," said Grenfell.

"It's better for us to enjoy our dinner and talk politics after," said Grieve.

"But you never answered my question, " persisted Paddon.

"You had better eat your dinner first because what I've got to tell you may not go down well on an empty stomach."

Paddon said no more.

Following dinner, they continued their conversation.

"I'll tell you now what you wanted to know," said Grieve.

Paddon looked at the Scotsman and said, "You were going to tell me who is the commissioner heading the enquiry into the cooperatives in Labrador."

"Yes, I think I was," said Grieve.

Grenfell said nothing as he sipped his tea and looked back and forth at each man.

"I can't say it is written in stone but we found out from our connections in St. John's that the fish merchants have chosen their man, and of course they run the government so it's up to them," said Grieve.

Paddon waited patently for Grieve to spill the beans.

"Magistrate Penney will be heading the enquiry, according to Job." (William Carson Job was a well respected gentleman and a St. John's merchant. He was also on the board of directors of the International Grenfell Association.)

Hearing that, Paddon's mouth fell open and he started to cuss.

"I don't believe you, John," he said. "No one would allow that to happen."

"I never thought the fish merchants had the nerve to try such tactics," said Grieve.

"Gentlemen," said Grenfell, holding up his hand. "We all knew that sooner or later the fish merchants were going to kick up because people are beginning to see what is going on. People want their justice, especially the fishermen coming to Labrador from the island who have been robbed of everything."

"I am shocked to say the least," said Paddon.

"Do you have any plan to try and have this stopped?" Grieve asked Grenfell.

"We're trying to find out what is going on in the House of Assembly, and after we get more facts we're going to act on them," said Grenfell.

"I know what I'm going to do," said Paddon. "I'm going to write Prime Minister Morris and ask him right out if he's chosen Penney to head the enquiry."

"No, I wouldn't do that if I were you," said Grenfell.

"Why not?"

Grenfell paused for a moment's thought. "I've got some very confidential information from someone I prefer not to identify, that Morris won't be Prime Minister for much longer, and if that's the case it will be in our favour," he said.

"How reliable is this information, Wilfred?" asked Grieve as he and Paddon looked at Grenfell in surprise.

"It is fact, gentleman, it will happen sometime after the New Year. He is going to be promoted to Baron Morris and will be going to England as a member of the War Cabinet in London."

Paddon laughed. "I wonder who will be replacing him?" he asked. It was obvious he did not like Morris because the Prime Minister hadn't acted on his promise to put pressure on the fish merchants to improve the scandalous way they were treating the fishermen.

"I hope it will be the Colonial Secretary, Richard Squires," said Grieve.

Grenfell laughed. "It will be William Lloyd, of course," he said. "He's now the acting Prime Minister. The decision has been made but not yet made public."

Paddon couldn't believe his ears. "Are you sure you know what you are talking about?" he asked.

"Yes, Harry, I certainly do. I heard it from the horse's mouth himself, Governor Davidson."

"I think this is very good news, gentlemen, although I would prefer Squires over Lloyd," said Paddon. "But at least now we will have someone who will probably listen to us because I know Lloyd personally."

"Not so fast," said Grieve. "If they have already made the decision to put Penney in charge of the enquiry it's too late for us to even try to do anything about it."

"I'll find that out as soon as I get back to St. John's. I'm going there next week, weather permitting, of course," said Grenfell.

"But Wilfred, as you know, a lot of things can be done in a week that can't be undone, and if the Cabinet happens to make Penney the commissioner of the enquiry it will be too late for us to do anything about it," said Paddon.

"I don't think Prime Minister Morris will create this problem for us and then walk away and leave it without first contacting me, as much as the fish merchants would like it if he did."

Grieve sat listening. He had been mad ever since a couple of days ago at Battle Harbour when Customs Officer Alex Simms told him the decision was already made and that Penney had been chosen as the commissioner.

"Wilfred," he said, "we should do something about this immediately, or at least get something straightened out."

"How about if we send Morris a telegram telling him not to accept Magistrate Penney as the commissioner for the enquiry?" said Paddon.

"The fish merchants have enough power to have Morris make that decision before he leaves unless we kick up a fuss first. If you are not prepared to do something about it now, then we are," said Grieve, pointing to himself and Paddon.

"I'll send a wireless to the Prime Minister tomorrow morning asking him for information about the enquiry and have him schedule a meeting with me next week in St. John's," said Grenfell.

The others were pleased he would do this. However, they were concerned about what would happen if Morris said it was already decided that Penney would be the commissioner.

"We'll wait to get a reply from Morris then we can decide what course of action to take," said Grenfell. "I'll keep you informed about what is going on. I'll send you both a copy of the Prime Minister's reply as soon as I get one."

Paddon let Grenfell know he would not wait very long, especially after hearing about what was happening on the political scene. But it was agreed they would all wait for a reply.

(As it happened, the decision to have Prime Minister Patrick Morris move to the War Cabinet in London was postponed for a year; it didn't happen until December 1917. Not even the members of Morris's cabinet knew he was going to resign until it happened.)

Archibald Piccott kept pressing for Morris to make the move on appointing a commissioner for the enquiry, namely Magistrate Penney.

However, Morris wasn't going to create a mess and run away and leave it to members of the House of Assembly to fight over something he had done while in office, especially something concerning Dr. Grenfell.

Morris immediately wired Grenfell and informed him no decision had been made about a commissioner and gave him the date for their meeting at St. John's.

Meanwhile, Piccott was in Morris's office daily for business discussions, and just about every day he would bring up the topic of what was going on with the "Grenfell co-ops." That was the phrase he used when discussing the cooperative stores in Labrador.

Morris stalled any action on the subject but was determined to have matters settled before he left office.

If members of his government had known Morris was soon going to be replaced they would have pressured him for immediate action on the Grenfell file.

CHAPTER 18
Winter 1917

The winter of 1917 was a troublesome time for the Colony of Newfoundland. World War I was continuing and more Newfoundlanders were being killed on the battlefields of Europe. Archibald Piccott and Walter Grieve and the other co-signers of the petition knew it wouldn't be wise to put forth such a document during the winter of 1917. They decided to postpone the project of tackling Dr. Grenfell and his Mission until spring.

In the early spring of 1917, fishermen got ready for the summer fishery along the coast. Skippers and crews loaded fishing gear and supplies into schooners and headed out by the thousands. The Census shows that more than 20,000 people went to the Labrador in 1917.

Fishing schooners were filled with women, children, and animals such as sledge dogs, sheep and goats. Captains of some vessels even carried a "milk cow," as they called them, to ensure a fresh supply of milk during the summer.

These people were not at all concerned about the cooperatives springing up along the coast. They were glad it was happening. What made them mad was that the floating and on-shore merchants to whom they sold their catches wouldn't pay them cash like the co-ops were doing.

Every fishing skipper was now talking about getting cash instead of going by the barter system. Seeing cash in the hands of ordinary fishermen who were selling to the co-ops, they were not satisfied with the fish merchant's way of "take out and turn in."

In most cases, before the fishermen left their home ports around Conception Bay and other places in Newfoundland, there was a lot of talk about being paid in cash for their fish. One fishing skipper going to Indian Tickle, Labrador, was heard to say, "This summer, I'm finally able to take my wife and family with me because Dr. Grenfell and his medical doctors are down there. What a blessing."

Everyone was aware that medical attention was available down on the Labrador because Dr. Grenfell was there.

The people of Conception Bay knew full well what poor medical treatment was all about. Just a couple of years earlier, tuberculosis was rampant. At the height of the outbreak, when many people were dying, Archibald Piccott, the area MHA, was asked to contact Dr. Rendell, the medical officer responsible for the treatment of tuberculosis on the Avalon Peninsula, and ask him to help.

Piccott wrote to Rendell, saying: "There are some very bad cases of tuberculosis here. I understand that a tuberculosis nurse has called on these people and left them only a pocket-handkerchief and a sputum cup. Then she gave them a lecture which they had to listen to on an empty stomach. Now my belief is that too much revenue has been spent on these lectures…And poor creatures who are dying daily, and have no nourishment and no medicine, are not fit subjects for the above treatment."

Rendell wrote to Colonial Secretary R. Watson, saying there were 10,000 cases of tuberculosis on the island of Newfoundland alone. He stressed that people weren't getting the proper nourishing food to help fight off disease. He said too that in the Bay Roberts district there wasn't necessary funding to treat people dying of tuberculosis.

The situation was such that many people were sick even before they left to go to Labrador for the summer fishery. So, the 20,000 souls setting off to prosecute the cod fishery were overjoyed to know that Grenfell and his team of doctors and nurses were waiting down north to meet their medical needs. "God help the man or men who would dare lay a finger on the medical work that Grenfell was doing down there," was their thinking.

The fish merchants were so obsessed with trying to put a halt to the cooperative movement that they really never thought about whose side the fishermen were on; they just plunged head on trying to get the government of the day to kick Dr. Grenfell and his Medical Mission out of the Colony.

Around the middle of December 1916, Dr. Grenfell went to St. John's and directly to Government House where Governor Walter Edward Davidson was expecting him.

The two main topics of conversation were the Great War raging in Europe and the unrest between fish merchants and the colonial government for allowing co-ops to exist in the North.

Grenfell asked if a commissioner had been named to carry out an enquiry for the fish merchants into allegations against the Grenfell Mission.

The Governor assured him that no such commissioner had been put in place, and said if there was he would be the first to know about it.

"Nothing has come to the floor of the House of Assembly yet concerning these allegations. There's been a lot of talk between members, but no action as of yet," he said.

Grenfell plunged in. "We feel there is one person who should not be put in charge of the enquiry and that is Magistrate Penney," he said. "He may be in a conflict of interest due to his years spent in Labrador as an agent for the fish merchants."

The Governor laughed. "You're not the first one to say that to me, but if the Cabinet approves him I won't have much of a choice. It will be either accept their approval or dissolve the government."

Grenfell knew this was going to be a major problem and he would have to tread very carefully.

The Governor leaned over in his chair and whispered, "Nothing will happen until Morris leaves office and Lloyd takes over sometime in the New Year."

Grenfell was glad to hear that, but he was still uneasy about what might happen.

Once the summer codfishery got into full swing and the agents for the fish merchants got settled in their summer quarters along the Labrador Coast and around the Northern Peninsula, there were rumours galore about the enquiry.

One favourite subject was how Magistrate Penney would fix up with the Grenfell crowd when he got started.

Dr. Paddon had moved to Indian Harbour in early spring and set up the summer hospital. When fishermen started arriving from Newfoundland, many came to his hospital for treatment, and of course the talk was about how the fish merchants had Magistrate Penney all geared up to boot the Grenfell Mission out of Labrador. Paddon became furious, convinced there was something to the rumours.

"The fish merchant government is hiding something from Dr. Grenfell. I think they've made their decision and are getting ready to spring a trap on us any day," he said to the hospital staff.

He decided to try and find out what was going by writing to Colonial Secretary Richard Squires.

In late July, he wrote Squires, requesting information on the pending enquiry, and asking who the commissioner was going to be. He said it was rumoured the fish merchants had already put Magistrate Penney in place.

Paddon wrote in such haste he forgot to sign his letter. That resulted in Squires sending the letter back to the Grenfell Mission at Indian Harbour asking who had written it.

CHAPTER 19

Ready for a Fight

In early June 1917, Walter Grieve went down to Battle Harbour on the first mail steamer going north. He wanted to visit his fishing and retail business before the start of the fishing season.

Upon arrival, he met his manager, John Croucher, and went directly to the office to talk over upcoming summer business. All he heard from Croucher was doom and gloom. The only thing he had on his mind was the co-op and the "Grenfell crowd" as he called them. He told Grieve a large shipment of duty free clothing had come in for the Grenfell Mission on the same coastal boat that he'd arrived on.

Walter asked if the clothing went to the co-op.

"I'm not sure where it went, it could have gone to the hospital," said Croucher." But it may have gone to the co-op. I saw people carrying bales of something over there."

Walter Grieve was very upset.

"Don't tell me anything else because I'm not in any mood for a quarrel this evening, enough has gone wrong already. I thought things would get a little better after Dr. Curtis took over here from John Grieve," he said.

(Dr. John Grieve was now the business manager for the International Grenfell Association in St. John's.)

That night, Walter went to bed in Battle Harbour a very angry man.

Walter couldn't stay at Battle Harbour. He had to get back to St. John's. The House of Assembly was about to have a spring session to pass bills pertaining to the railway.

As well, he'd received a wireless message from Mr. Wood, lawyer for the fish merchants, saying that they were presenting a petition to the House of Assembly and asking for the enquiry on June 12, 1917. Walter wanted to be present for that.

On the coastal boat, all he'd heard about was how people wanted to get paid in cash for their fish and were going to demand receipts for everything they sold. He told Croucher this was the beginning of the end for his firm.

The way he saw it, the co-op was in full swing and free clothing was being given out to anyone who wanted it. For those reasons, he came back to St. John's ready for a fight.

CHAPTER 20

Judge Squarey Appointed

U p until this date the government had not even considered
naming a commissioner to head the enquiry for the
simple reason it had not been presented on the floor of the
House of Assembly.

There was a lot of talk about who the fish merchants wanted,
namely Magistrate Penney. Every politician had discussed the
issue. Some disagreed with having Penney as commissioner, but
most wanted him.

They used the argument that he was the only judge
experienced with court cases in Labrador and that he knew all the
people and the goings on along the coast, especially about the
cooperatives.

The Prime Minister, Mr. Morris, and the Governor, Edward
Davidson, were determined not to allow Penney to head the
enquiry.

"The only judge in the Colony capable of heading this enquiry
is Judge Robert Squarey," said the Prime Minister.

"Why is that?" asked the Governor.

"Squarey is someone who is independent and not biased
toward anyone, he will tell it like it is," said Morris.

"The members of the House may not go along with Squarey.
Most of them seem to want Penney," said the Governor.

"I think they'll be satisfied with Squarey because of his
reputation," said the Prime Minister.

After a long conversation between the two men it was decided
that they would contact Judge Robert T. Squarey Esq. of Channel,
Port Aux Basques, and ask him if he would head the enquiry.

On August 3, 1917, William F. Lloyd, who was acting Prime Minister and acting Attorney General, wrote Judge Squarey the following letter:

Government of Newfoundland
Colonial Building
St. John's
Office of the Attorney General

3rd August 1917

To Judge R. T. Squarey
Stipendiary Magistrate,
Channel, Port-Aux-Basques, NFLD

Sir:
The Government has decided to have an enquiry held into certain allegations made in the petition presented to the Legislature some few weeks ago by Messrs. John Rorke & Sons and others, in reference to the operations of the International Grenfell Association of America.

I may say that the Association have intimated to the Prime Minister, the Rt. Hon. Sir E. P. Morris, P.C., K.C.M.G., their desire that such an enquiry be held.

I have been directed to ask whether you are prepared to conduct such an enquiry.

If so, will you kindly let me know immediately and a Commission of enquiry will be made out to you.

I enclose herewith a copy of the petition presented to the Honourable the House of Assembly, in order that you may be acquainted with the scope of the enquiry, which will be limited to the charges and allegations contained in the petition.

I have the Honour to be,
Sir, Your obedient servant,
William F. Lloyd,
Acting Attorney General

The following is a copy of the fish merchant's petition as sent to Squarey:

To the Honourable the House of Assembly in Legislative Session convened.

The Petition of the undersigned Humbly Sheweth: —

1. *That your Petitioners are engaged in the mercantile business of the Colony and have large undertakings on the coast of Labrador.*

2. *That competition is very keen where so many rival interests are involved.*

3. *That for many years your petitioners have silently acquiesced in the competition of charitable organizations in the interest of the poorer class of fishermen who have derived benefits there from.*

4. *That on misrepresentations that this dependency of Newfoundland is largely composed of paupers, the charity of the generous people of the United States has been greatly stimulated and the benefits in money and kind have been so largely increased that they have now become a menace to all other mercantile concerns on that coast that have to pay duty and freight upon the material they use or vend in the prosecution of the fisheries there.*

5. *That the privileges heretofore extended to the International Grenfell Association of America, successors to the Royal Mission to deep sea Fishermen should either be sensibly curtailed or abolished not only on account of the above reasons but seeing that it is affiliated to certain stores trading on the coast and thereby they have an outlet for the sail of duty free merchandise introduced under the caption of goods for charitable purposes.*

6. *That your petitioners have reason to believe that these stores are capitalized by American Philanthropists who have interest without any idea of receiving dividend or interest.*

7. *That this is no mere assumption as evidence exist that the Customs Authorities have detected breaches of the Law and have compelled payment to be made by the Association.*

Your petitioners therefore humbly pray that your Honourable House will cause enquiry to be made as to the correctness of these allegations with a view to there removal or remedy.

And as in duty bound your petitioners will humbly pray.

St. John's, NF.
12 June 1917

The merchants who signed the petition were: Messrs. John Rorke & Sons; William Duff & Sons Limited per R, Duff, director; J.J.Maddock; Joseph Udell & Sons; W.H. Soper; Baine Johnston & Company; R.D. McRae & Sons and James Cron.

CHAPTER 21

Addition to Petition

When the petition was introduced to the House of Assembly it became a public document. Dr. Grenfell was notified when this happened and also sent a copy of the petition.

The Governor immediately invited Grenfell and his officials to come to St. John's for a meeting. Dr. Grenfell and Dr. John Grieve went to the office of Sir Walter Davidson, accompanied by Mr. William C. Job, a member of the board of directors of the International Grenfell Association of America (IGA), and Newfoundland's ambassador to the United States.

It was quite a meeting to say the least.

The Governor wasn't sure how this was going to affect the Grenfell organization along the Labrador Coast. He was also puzzled how it was going to be handled in the House of Assembly because members connected with the fishery could stack it.

Dr. John Grieve was not very happy. He was so fed up with what was happening he was ready to throw in the towel and head back to Scotland. (Grieve did resign after the enquiry was complete. He could not take any more.)

Grenfell spoke before Grieve could make a statement.

"Gentleman, I would like to say something please. If we could add one sentence to that petition, then it would be the best thing that happened to our operation since we arrived in the Colony in 1892."

The Governor and Dr. Grieve looked at Grenfell with a puzzled look and signaled for him to continue.

Grenfell reached into his pocket and took out a small piece of paper folded not much bigger then his thumb.

He opened it and read out the words typed on it: "*To report generally on the work of the Association and to what extent and in what way that work is a public benefit.*"

He folded the paper and put it back into his shirt pocket. "If we can get this sentence added to the petition then we will be satisfied for the enquiry to go ahead," he said then paused and added, "If the government won't allow the sentence to be added we will cause a lot of trouble for the Colony."

"Listen, Wilfred," said Grieve, "the crowd at Government House is so powerful I don't think we'll ever be able to do them any harm."

"Don't be too sure about that, John," said Grenfell.

Grieve was anxious to hear what could be done to put a halt to the goings-on. Grenfell looked at the Governor, and then at Job, who was listening quietly to the conversation.

"Before I came to this meeting, the ambassador and I had a lengthy meeting about the contents of the petition and what damage it could do to the Colony if it wasn't done properly," said Grenfell. "As you know, Mr. Job has a lot of close friends in Washington and so do I. If the Prime Minister and his Cabinet are not willing to add the wording I just read to the petition, then we will make it known to every fish merchant in this Colony that we will ask Washington to boycott every fish that goes south of St. Pierre."

The Governor raised his eyebrows, he could hardly believe what he was hearing.

"Good God in heaven, Wilfred, do you know what you are saying?" he asked.

Grenfell had the attention of the most powerful man in the Colony and he intended to keep it.

"We are not asking that the government cancel the enquiry, on the contrary, we welcome the enquiry to a point, that is if the Prime Minister will add the sentence I just read," said Grenfell. "If the sentence doesn't go in, then there will be serious trouble."

"And that's not all," said Job as he looked at the Governor. "I will go personally to every fisherman, and there are 25,000 who go down north every summer, and tell them that they can sell their fish directly to foreign boats and get a better price right from their stage heads and that this can be done in every fishing community."

There was a silence as Governor Davidson stood up and walked across the room. This man was no fool, he knew when people were serious. He knew this was very serious business.

"In order for you to get any changes to the petition, you will have to write a letter to the Cabinet requesting the petition be cancelled and a new one drawn up and presented in its place, putting in the changes that you want made," said the Governor.

"I agree fully," said Grenfell.

"What if the Cabinet doesn't agree? Is there another way we can go about it?" asked Grieve.

"Yes, there is another way," said Grenfell.

"What is it?" asked the Governor.

"I have a file in my office that is marked 'extremely confidential' that no one has seen, not even my wife. It contains letters from the Premier of British Columbia and the Prime Minister of Canada asking me to come to British Columbia to do the same work among their people as we have done here. And that's not all. The Government of Canada is willing to finance the complete exodus of every living soul now living on the Labrador Coast to British Columbia the minute we give the word."

Governor Davidson was silent. He appeared to be in a state of shock. He knew Grenfell wasn't lying.

Even Job and Grieve were shocked, but they knew Grenfell had an ace in the hole that could cause enough trouble to set the Colony back economically for years.

Davidson sat at his desk and looked at Grenfell. "What you have there is powerful stuff, Wilfred," he said.

The room was silent.

"I will take the matter up with Prime Minister Morris tonight when we have a dinner meeting. We are supposed to discuss the war tax proposal. I will add this to the agenda," said the Governor. He concluded by saying to Grenfell, "I want you to come here tomorrow at 11 a.m. I will let you know then what Mr. Morris had to say about the matter. I would like you to bring Mr. Watson with you (Robert Watson was the director of the IGA for Newfoundland and a member of the international board). I can fill him in on what the Prime Minister has to say about the matter."

Grenfell agreed to come to the meeting with Mr. Watson.

At their meeting the next day, the Governor told them that the Prime Minister had advised him to tell Mr. Watson to write him personally about what they would like to see changed in the petition, and to also request the Prime Minister to appoint a commissioner to look at the work being done by the Grenfell Association.

"Mr. Morris advised that he would be out of his office until July 25. He said you should make sure that your letter is hand-delivered to him personally sometime after that."

Dr. Grenfell and Robert Watson thanked the Governor and left Government House. That was June 18, 1917.

CHAPTER 22
Letter to Prime Minister

I t is not recorded, and I suppose it will never be known what
went on and what was said during the meetings that Dr.
Grenfell held concerning the fight to get the petition changed.
We only know what was written and recorded and conversations
that were exchanged by credible people close to the Grenfell
people at the time. However, in our research, we found the
following letter that was hand delivered to the Prime Minister:

The International Grenfell Association
INCORPORATED

SUPERINTENDENT: WILFRED T. GRENFELL. M.D C.M.G.

St. John's. Newfoundland,
July 21, 1917

Dear Sir Edward:

*As you are aware, a petition was lately presented to the House
of Assembly from Messrs. Baine Johnston & Company of this city
and others, in relation to the charitable works carried on in
Northern Newfoundland and in Labrador by the International
Grenfell Association.*

The petitioners allege that the custom privileges granted to the Association have been abused by the use in trade of goods given for charitable purposes; and that the Cooperatives stores conducted by fishermen in localities where the Association operates are capitalized by American philanthropists connected with the Association who invest their money without hope of dividends or interest, thus unfairly competing with the business of the petitioners; and they ask for an investigation and for the curtailment of the privileges granted by the Government to the Association and its predecessors in this work.

I desire on behalf of the Association to ask if the Government can see its way to appoint a suitable Commission or Commissioner and authorizing them or him to conduct an enquiry of a scope and thoroughness commensurate with the importance of the work the Association is now doing in Newfoundland and Labrador.

We ask that the powers of the Commission be not limited to the investigation of the specific charges of illegal conduct made by the Petitioners. If the enquiry is to ascertain whether the Governmental assistance given the Association ought to be reduced, it should also, we submit, be open to the Commission, if it's findings so warrant, to recommend that the assistance be increased; and if the Commission had power to report that the Association's work is fair, as the petitioner's suggest, a menace to the public welfare, it should also be prepared to report, if such is the fact, in what was and to what extent that the work is a public benefit.

We ask, in brief, that an exhaustive enquiry be made into the character and merits of the Association generally with the Government and with the people. Every possible facility, both here and at the Hospital stations, will be offered to the person or persons appointed. We have absolute confidence that upon any impartial enquiry the work of the Association will speak for itself; and in our own interest as well as the public interest we urge the immediate appointment of a commission of Enquiry, so that the summer season may be availed of, for a visit to St. Anthony and Labrador.

Yours faithfully,
Robert Watson.
Director,
International Grenfell Association, Inc.

The Right Honourable
Sir Edward Morris, P.C., K.C.M.G.,
Prime Minister

CHAPTER 23
Judge Squarey

J udge Robert Squarey was the senior magistrate in the Colony
   and very well respected. When he received the letter from
   William Lloyd asking him to conduct an enquiry into the
operations of the International Grenfell Association as requested
by the fish merchants, he talked it over with his wife before
agreeing to take on the job. He then sent the following telegram to
Lloyd:

*7 Aug 1917 instant received, am in your hands, place me
where I can best serve the Country. Stop.*
*Manslaughter case here waiting re-sitting of the Supreme
Court. Stop.*
My presence not absolutely necessary. Stop.
Please advise. Stop.
Robert R. Squarey

Magistrate Squarey was an Englishman married to a woman
from Harbour Grace. They lived in a nice house at Channel, Port
aux Basques. Mrs. Squarey had no intention of staying alone while
her husband was away on an enquiry. It was decided she would go
to Harbour Grace and stay with her parents while he conducted the
enquiry.

After he agreed to be the commissioner and received a copy of
the petition from Attorney General Lloyd, Judge Squarey found it
to be somewhat one-sided. He had met the famous Labrador
doctor, Wilfred Grenfell, and admired his work. He had heard
about the cooperative movement and the duty free clothing

coming to the Grenfell Mission from the United States and Canada for the poor. But now, he was being asked to investigate the sale of these goods to the poor. What really puzzled him was that if the Grenfell Association was selling duty free clothing to the poor, where were the poor getting the cash to buy it? On August 5, 1917, Governor Davidson sent the following letter to Judge Squarey:

DRAFT COMMISSION.

By his Excellency Sir Walter Edward Davidson, etc., etc.

To:

Robert R. Squarey, Esq., J.P.,

Greetings:

WHEREAS a petition has been presented to the House of Assembly by certain persons engaged in the mercantile business of the Colony, and having large undertakings on the coast of Labrador, praying that enquiry be made as to correctness of the following allegations, with a view to their removal or remedy:

That for many years petitioners have silently acquiesced in the competition of charitable organizations in the interest of the poorer class of fishermen, who have derived benefits there from.
That on misrepresentation that this Dependency of Newfoundland is largely composed of paupers the charity of the generous people of the United States has been greatly stimulated, and the benefits in money and kind have been so largely increased that they have now become a menace to all other mercantile concerns on that coast, who have to pay duty and freight upon materials they use or vend in the prosecution of the fisheries there.

That the privileges heretofore extended to the International Grenfell Association of America, successors to the Royal Mission to Deep Sea Fishermen, should either be reasonably curtailed or abolished, not only on account of the above reasons, but seeing that it is affiliated to certain stores trading on the coast, and thereby they have an outlet for the sale of duty free merchandise introduced under the caption of "Goods for Charitable purposes".

Those Petitioners have reason to believe that American philanthropists who have invested without any idea of receiving dividend or interest capitalize these stores.

And WHEREAS I deem it expedient that an enquiry should be made concerning the allegations contained in the aforementioned petition. I do, therefore, by these Presents, nominate and appoint you, the said Robert T. Squarey, to be Commissioner, under and by virtue of Chapter 30, of the Consolidate Statues of Newfoundland, Second Series, entitled, "Of Enquiries Concerning Public Matters," to enquire into and report to me concerning the aforesaid charges and allegations and any matters that may arise out of the same during the process of the enquiry, and which you consider should be inquired into, conferring upon you, the said Robert T. Squarey, the power of summoning before you any party or witness, and of requiring such party or witness to give witness on oath, either orally or in writing (or upon solemn affirmation), and to produce such documents and things as you may deem requisite to the full investigation of the matters into which you are appointed to examine.

Given under my hand and seal,
At the Government House,
St. John's, this 5th day of August, A.D. 1917

Sir Walter Davidson,
Governor

CHAPTER 24

Commotion Started

After the Governor appointed Judge Squarey commissioner there was quite a commotion between Prime Minister Morris and the petitioners. They were very disappointed that Judge Penney hadn't been selected. But it was pointed out that the Governor had the power to appoint whomever he wanted in such a matter as this. 'You have no other choice but to accept the appointment," Morris told the petitioners and Piccott, who was then no longer the Minister of Marine and Fisheries.

In a meeting that Piccott attended with Walter Grieve and the petitioners, it was argued that because Squarey was an Englishman and Governor Davidson was an Irishman and a British civil servant, they would side with Grenfell.

The lawyers doubted it would happen because the newspapers would be reporting on everything that happened. Prime Minister Morris would also be watching the enquiry closely as he was concerned about the merchants' threat of boycotting the fishery along the Labrador Coast.

On August 10, 1917, Attorney General Lloyd wrote to the Colonial Secretary, Richard Squires, and informed him that he had heard back from Judge Squarey and the judge had agreed to conduct the enquiry. In Mr. Lloyd's letter he stated:

"I understand the scope of the enquiry will be limited to the matters in the petition of John Rourke & Sons and others. From Mr. Squarey's reply you will see that he is prepared to conduct the Enquiry. Kindly have the usual Commission made out to Mr. Squarey. I am notifying him to come to St. John's by Monday's train.

W.F. Lloyd
Acting Attorney General

On August 13, the Colonial Secretary wrote the Minister of Justice advising him that there would be a correction made to the wording of the enquiry. He also enclosed the papers concerning the changes to be made on the matter. On August 17, Governor Davidson wrote to Judge Squarey and informed him that the terms of the enquiry would be changed. He instructed him to return the petition he had and a new one would be issued to him.

This did not surprise Judge Squarey after seeing the one-sidedness of the petition. He wrote back to the Governor thanking him for his letter, and advised him that he was anxiously awaiting the draft of the new petition.

The following letter was sent to Colonial Secretary Richard Squires from the Minister of Justice on the same date:

Sir:
I beg to return herewith Commission issued to Magistrate Squarey in the matter of the Grenfell Enquiry, a new Commission enlarging the scope of the enquiry having been sent to him a couple of days ago.

W. F. Lloyd
Minister of Justice

Between August 17 and September 1, there must have been a lot of arguing back and forth between the Government and the petitioners. However, with the war raging in Europe and the fishery in full swing around the coast, it was thought this was the best time to put through changes to the petition. And this is what the Government did, after first adding the lines proposed by Grenfell.

When Walter Grieve heard about the changes through the grapevine he was very angry. He called a meeting with the lawyers and Arch Piccott and a few more of the petitioners. After hours of discussion, it was concluded it was futile and a waste of time to have the enquiry.

Archibald Piccott was called to Government House for a meeting with Governor Davidson. When he arrived, he found the Honourable William Job sitting at the table with the Governor.

Now it is to be noted that Walter Davidson was not softhearted nor was he easily pushed around. He was not fond of the tactics used by the fish merchants in their dealings with fishermen in Labrador. He was also a close friend of the Reverend Moses Harvey, who had been instrumental in having the British Government send Dr. Grenfell to Newfoundland.

And to say the least, Piccott was no pussycat himself, he cared for nothing or no one. When he walked into Government House and saw Job sitting there he didn't quake with fear.

He shook hands with the Governor and with Job and sat down, just as a maid in a white apron pushed a trolley loaded with a sterling silver coffee container and the finest china that money could buy into the room.

Governor Davidson had a reputation for debating issues, and had proved it on several occasions while he was Mayor of Colombo at the turn of the century. He was 58 years old and known as a fiery Irishman.

"We won't beat around the bush one little bit, Arch," he said as he tasted the black coffee. It was obvious he had something he wanted to get off his chest.

After the girl had poured coffee and placed a plate of tea biscuits on the table, she very gently closed the large doors behind her as she left.

"Walter, what's on the mind of the Irishman today?" Piccott asked the Governor as he tapped his teaspoon on the table.

"We should be talking about the war, Arch," said the Governor. "But this mess about the Grenfell racket has even got the war in Europe overshadowed. To tell you the truth, I haven't heard anything like it. Even keeps me awake at night."

Piccott said nothing as he waited for the Governor to continue.

"What's this I hear Arch, about Walter Grieve and his petitioners going down on the Labrador and around northern Newfoundland and trying to turn the fishermen against the Grenfell Mission and the Government?"

Job sat quietly and waited for Piccott to answer. When Piccott didn't answer, Governor Davidson continued.

"Just imagine Arch, some fellow down there on the Labrador with something in his eye for a couple of days and they take him to one of the Grenfell doctors or nurses and get it taken out. Another person with the toothache for days, they take him to the Grenfell people to get his teeth pulled. Some sick child or a sick mother, maybe on the hand of dying, they take them to the Grenfell doctor and they get better," he paused then said, "You're going to go around and get people to ask the Government to shut down the hospitals and nursing stations just because the fish merchants are mad because they're starting co-ops or selling some clothes."

Arch didn't answer. He looked at Job who was watching the Governor with keen interest.

"Arch, I am surprised to hear you told one of your close friends you agreed with the petitioners doing such a stupid thing," said the Governor. He reached into his desk and took out a copy of the Act of the Statues of the Colony of Newfoundland. "Do you know they could be charged with a serious offense?" he asked, looking at Piccott again. "The whole crowd could be charged with attempting to start a riot. That calls for an automatic jail sentence. They could be arrested…I don't know what that crowd wants to do, unless it is to destroy all our creditably and leave us with nothing."

Arch Piccott was not afraid of the Governor and he knew it. Arch cleared his throat and leaned over with his elbows on the table. "When you're finished talking, I have something to say," he said.

"I'm finished, go ahead," said the Governor.

"I'm not part of a group who want to drive Grenfell off the Labrador. I'm not one of the petitioners either."

The Governor was not to be fooled.

"Explain to us what they're intending to do if the commissioner rules in their favour?" he asked.

"Every name on that petition wants to see a stop put to what the Grenfell crowd is doing in regard to starting cooperatives down on the Labrador. They want to see a stop put to selling goods that have been donated to them, that have come into this country duty free."

The Governor tried to butt in, but Arch held up his hand.

"Just a minute Walter, you had your say, now I'm going to have mine," he said. "Can't you see what's happening? Every business down north is being destroyed just because a bunch of doctors are telling the people they can offer them a better way of life when they can't."

"That's not what it's all about, Arch," said Job.

Piccott turned to Job. "What is it all about, William?" he asked.

Job cleared his throat. "None of this would have happened if you hadn't got a black eye down at Battle Harbour last year," he said.

Arch didn't like that reference one little bit.

He turned to Job with eyes blazing. "What are you trying to tell me, that I'm the cause of all this?" he asked.

Job was a soft-spoken man, but when he spoke he spoke with authority. "The word is being circulated, or might I say being whispered between friends, that you started it all, Arch," he said.

Arch turned to the Governor. "As far as the fish merchants are concerned, the enquiry is finished anyway. When the House changed the wording of the petition it was changed to favour the Grenfell Mission," he said.

"It was one-sided Arch, you know that, the law wouldn't allow it to go ahead as it was, so we changed it," said the Governor.

"Look Walter," said Arch, "half of the petitioners say they won't even go to the court house to testify. If they're forced to go they say they won't give any evidence because they're frightened." Arch paused then added, "Take me for instance, if I'm forced to go on the stand, I won't be saying anything because I'm afraid."

"They will go on the stand Arch, and give evidence. They signed the petition."

Piccott knew the Governor was right, the petitioners could be arrested and brought to the courthouse in handcuffs if need be.

"I think I am leaving sir," Arch said to the Governor, as he stepped away from the table. As he turned to go he said, "There's one thing I want to say to you before I leave."

"Go ahead, Arch, you can say whatever you like, now's your chance."

"You may have all the authority here in the Colony, but I would like to say that some of the fish merchants who've got their names signed to that petition have a lot of friends in London and other high places. When this is over you could see some changes. Even you could go."

The Governor said nothing else because he knew Arch Piccott was at a boiling point. With that, the Governor picked up the papers on the table in front of him and walked back into the parlour, closing the door behind him.

Piccott looked at William Job, shook his head, and left Government House. (It is to be noted that Governor Walter Davidson left Newfoundland shortly after the enquiry ended and was transferred to New South Wales.)

Piccott went straight to the office of Walter Grieve. He marched into his office without knocking and shut the door behind him with a bang.

Walter was startled. He'd been studying some papers and hadn't looked up when the door opened, thinking it was his secretary. When the door banged shut, his head shot up.

"Arch," he said, dropping his pen in surprise.

"Yes, it's me, and I'm out of my mind with rage."

"You sure look like it and it doesn't look good," said Walter. "I've just come from a meeting with the Governor. I tried to get hold of you earlier but you were out."

"What did Davidson want to see you about?"

"He more or less told me that we're all in trouble for calling the enquiry. He said we could all end up in jail."

"So he frightened you, hey Arch," said Walter.

"No, he didn't frighten me, but when I told him that he could get kicked out of Newfoundland for changing the petition to suit the Grenfell crowd he almost boiled over."

"I've been talking to some people in London and explained to them what Davidson did with our petition. They're not very pleased," said Walter.

"I told him I wouldn't go to court to give evidence, and I won't."

"You'll be going to court, that's for sure Arch, whether in handcuffs or not that will be up to you. Whether you say anything more than yes or no is also up to you."

"I've never seen anything like this before, Walter. Grenfell has got more power then the Government. He's got them all on side." Arch sat down in a chair near the corner of Walter's overcrowded desk.

Walter looked at him, knowing he was frustrated about what was going on. "Let's have a drink," he said.

"Good idea," said Arch as Walter reached into his desk and took out a bottle of rum. He poured out half a glass and mixed it with water. Arch drank it down in two gulps.

Arch sat for a few minutes and said nothing. He tried to think of something he could get his teeth into but there was nothing. He no longer had access to the Prime Minister's office so getting there directly was out of the question. "We should all clamp up and refuse to go to the enquiry when we're called," he said.

This had been discussed with the lawyers a couple of days ago and the lawyers said the petitioners could be subpoenaed into court. It was up to them whether or not they gave evidence.

"Walter, have you got any angle we could use to get the wording changed back to what it was?" asked Arch.

"I'll be meeting with our lawyers again tonight. I'll ask them the same question," said Walter.

The two men said no more. In a few minutes Arch was gone.

The Colonial Secretary wrote the following letter to the Hon. Robert Watson, Director of the International Grenfell Association, St. John's:

Dear Sir:
Referring to your letter respecting the scope of the enquiry which is being made just now by Magistrate Squarey into certain allegations respecting the International Grenfell Association, I have the Honour to intimate that the Government directed that the Commission which was issued to Magistrate Squarey in this connection should be cancelled and a new Commission issued broadening the scope of the enquiry.

The new Commission has now gone to the Magistrate and there has been included this phrase.

{"To report generally on the work of the Association and to what extent and in what way that work is a public benefit"}

Which will enable the Magistrate to bring under review very much more then was set forth in the first Commission.

I have no doubt that this will be satisfactory to the International Grenfell Association.

> *Yours truly,*
> *Richard Squires.*

And so, with all the decks cleared away the enquiry began.

CHAPTER 25

Paddon's Letter

O n the 23 of August 1917, Paddon wrote Squires the following letter, containing much more information than his original unsigned one. Until this date, Dr. Paddon and the others down north were not aware Judge Squarey had been appointed commissioner for the enquiry. By the time Squires got to answer Paddon's letter regarding Squarey's appointment, the enquiry had already begun.

The International Grenfell Association
INCORPORATED

Superintendent: Wilfred T. Grenfell, M.D., and C.M.G.

Registered Office
King George the 5th Seaman's Institute
St. Johns, N.F.L.D.

Indian Harbour Labrador

CONFIDENTIAL

Aug. 23 1917

Dear Mr. Squires:
I am sorry for my careless error in not signing the letter re:
Defects in chartable administration.

I am wondering, very anxiously, whether you can see your way
to fulfilling the promise given by your predecessor to place an
able-bodied, intelligent, itinerant investigator on the coast this
winter, to look into conditions as they really are, and to report on
them with a view to reform.

We have recently been attacked once more in the
Newfoundland press as "falsely representing Labrador as a
pauper community," besides swindling the Customs etc. etc.
For over twenty years this sort of vapouring has gone on, Sir.
God knows we have nothing to fear from investigation; whereas
others have a good deal to fear, if the investigation were thorough
and unbiased.

Both parties have now demanded it, and my one fear is that it
will not go far enough.

Hitherto the practice has been to allow the guiltiest, the most
prejudiced, the most self-interested and the most ignorant parties
to give us the lie and disparage our reputations without any
further questions.

I hope for something different this time.

After six summers and four winters in this bay and the
neighborhood, my honest conviction is that Labrador has been to
valuable a dumping ground for the hungry dependents of party
politicians to be lightly reformed and allowed to develop.

At a time when economy and efficiency are so large a part of
patriotism, one looks to a Coalition Government, (surely with
reason) to disprove the "unholy alliance" the talk of Dr. Lloyd by
eradicating the following crying evils.

No. 1

> *To remedy Labrador's need for a keen, able, honest*　　　　＇
> *Commissioner (for Heaven's sake, spare us a nominal*
> *representative who knows nothing about the country or*
> *people), one of Newfoundland's best brains.*
> *After 110 years of Dependency without representation,*
> *employment, or more then a smattering of education or*
> *Justice, this is sadly overdue.*

No. 2

> *It is surely no more than common sense to state that, without*
> *organized industry, a community can hardly be otherwise than*
> *pauper.*
> *The sickening thing is that enough money has been wasted in*
> *promiscuous, unintelligent unsupervised "charity" to solve the*
> *whole problem.*

No. 3

> *In justification of my statement that Labrador is a political*
> *dumping ground, I urge:*
> *A. That Customs posts are double manned where there is not*
> *work for one e.g. An officer I could name has plenty of*
> *time to run a fishery for his own benefit, and yet has a*
> *salaried assistant!*
>
> *B. Even lighthouses are retained almost exclusively for*
> *Newfoundlanders, where Labrador men could give from*　＇
> *one to two more months service each year.*
>
> *C. The "traveling judge" still takes an annual rest cure on the*
> *outskirts of Labrador, while the big bays remain unexplored*
> *by him and teeming with lawlessness.*
> *The number of convictions and penalties enforced in five*
> *years could be of interest. These are generalities.*
> *When it comes to details, I have a good deal down in black*
> *and white, which is the reverse of creditable.*
> *The fact that I write confidentially proves my desire to try*
> *to get something done without a fuss.*

D. "Charity," perhaps the biggest scandal of all, I have written about before. I understand you referred it to the Department of Charities. Failing quick action, I see no recourse but to publish the facts and rely on the good sense of a patriotic public. Were I a freelance, I should have done this without bothering you. At present, Labrador being without a Government (to all intents and purposes) is not as patriotic as she should be. Such officials as there are do not appear, to the resident, to be chosen for enterprise, ability, or in some cases integrity. Some are said to be paid twelve months salary for 4-5 months work, which is largely imaginary. In the case of charity, not even accounts are kept of the expenditures of public money. To the most casual observer many inconsistencies are apparent. A game warden, who holds the position long after Mr. Rabbitts had declared him to be retired, a Fish Warden who issues "magistrate's injunctions" to detain people's goods to pay his own trading debts. A higher official who, according to signed and witnessed statements, issued liquor to Eskimos and whose public immorality is outrageous; these are the sort of things one longs to see disappear.

A capable, upright and public-spirited Commissioner could control or eradicate such defects, and Labrador might become a British Dependency in more then name.
As I write, a J.P. is accused of causing foxes to be poisoned. He is a fur trader. So far no one has seemed to care.
The public does not know how its money is wasted, and has been educated to regard any English gentlemen resident on the coast as fools, liars and swindlers, by those who are interested in maintaining a status quo.
I could mention one of our present opponents as charging 66% usury on a cash advance to a settler. When one of our staff starts a Cooperative store to abolish such oppression, he makes his counterblast.

We do not care so much what we are called, but we do want to see Labrador develop.

It is very little that one man, or even an Association, can do backed by private philanthropy when they are jealously watched and persistently slandered by certain merchants, and beset by nominal officials making hay while the sun shines, while those in authority care not whether they speak truth or lie.

I will just tell you what I am trying to do. With my superintendent's approval and the help of our supporters, to show that we are not merely destructive critics, but are tiding over the period of Labrador's anarchy, ready to fall in line with the first public spirited effort to work a reform by those who, so far, seem to have little use for us and none for the evolution of the Dependency.

In a few years I have had here, I have tried to tackle the poverty problem, to some extent, by letting Labrador men into the cod fishery. I have got over thirty either employed by Newfoundland skippers, who find them among their best men, or fishing independently.

This does certainly reduce the Government expenses and would be a natural work of any Commissioner worth his keep.

I have had the privilege of making a new 26 bed hospital here and getting a Cottage Hospital erected at the other end of the Bay.

While denominational red tape makes education very scanty and inferior, one minister (who does not consider me anathema because I am inter- denominational) is working with me to establish two small winter schools.

Personally, I am too bad a businessman to dabble in Cooperative stores, but I vividly realize the need of them.

We try to encourage agriculture and the raising of livestock amid a community who, despite all the babbling of prejudice and self-interested ignoramuses, are continually undernourished.

This is again the natural work of any Commissioner worth his salt.

You may have thought it small minded on my part to throw up my Justice's commission, but what was the use of it when:

1. *The Newfoundland Statute book was out of print during my entire tenure of office.*
2. *I had no legal training and had no one to consult. If I tried to get the 'rest-cure judge' he was off like a hunted hare - and if I caught him he knew little more then I.*
3. *The fish laws never reached me in time to be of any use. It was pure farce, not worth maintaining.*

You have always been kindly and courteous to our staff and I hope you will not resent this plain picture.

It may seem a presumptuous effort to dictate, but I wish it interpreted as a man-to-man talk by one patriotic Britain to another. What I plead for is investigation, at least, of the most backward of British possessions.

The colored races of Egypt and Nigeria are administered by first-rate men. Sir Frederick Lugard has reaped the harvest of years of able patriotic service, during this war. I realize Labrador is not of such strategic importance as African colonies, but I don't believe the least populous, the least productive, the least strategic, the least anything that is British deserves taxation without representation, and bogus exploitation without employment to say nothing of a collection of summer tripping officials whose services are certainly not in proportion to their remuneration, and resident ones of whom the less said, the better!

> *I remain*
> *Yours truly,*
> *H.L. Paddon*

P.S. Dr. Grenfell now has a mass of evidence, which I got wind of last winter, that "Justice Of The Peace" White is an adulterer, fornicator, a donor of liquor to Eskimos, and a poisoner of foxes for his own benefit as a trader.

He, like me, feels that no Englishman can be numbered as a colleague of White, Sheard and Gosse, and he, like myself, will throw up his commission as J.P. unless this type of official is changed on this coast.

The following is Mr. Squires' reply to Dr. Paddon:

September 18, 1917
Dr. H. L. Paddon
Indian Harbour, Labrador

Dear Mr. Paddon:

I have the pleasure to acknowledge the receipt of your letter of August 25th 1917, which I have read and re-read with much interest.

I think that the Association should be entirely satisfied with the standing and experience of the gentleman who has been appointed Commissioner.

Magistrate Squarey of Channel Port-aux-Basques was selected for many reasons.

He was as far removed from the controversy, which has taken place concerning the Grenfell Association and its work, as it is possible for a Newfoundlander to be. He is probably the senior Magistrate for the Colony, and has, on many past occasions been entrusted with important undertakings.

He is an Englishman of that sturdy type of independence, which has developed in him the characteristic of being absolutely square and straightforward.

He is not the type of man to jump to conclusions, or is influenced by trivialities, but one of the solid build that arrive at conclusions slowly but from opinions, which are valuable.

In addition to all this, he has an intimate knowledge of the northern section of Newfoundland, not as they are at present but as they were in days gone by.

He is not undertaking an investigation in connection with territory, the geography and topography of which he is unacquainted.

He is a good sailor, and the type of man who is prepared to overcome difficulties to make his investigation complete and thorough.

The Commission, which was first issued, called merely for an enquiry into the charges in the petition of those who first sought investigation.

The Commission has, however, been enlarged to full scope of enquiry by the Association in a communication received from the Association's solicitors.

I feel quite confident that Magistrate Squarey's investigation will be full and complete.

The young man who is his clerk and stenographer is a gentleman of high standing in the community.

He is a graduate of either Oxford or Cambridge, is the son of the Registrar of the Supreme Court, and will, within a very short period, qualify as a barrister of the Supreme Court of Newfoundland.

Your Association is selecting Mr. Charles E. Hunt to represent you in this investigation, and has made an exceedingly wise selection, in that Mr. Hunt's pleasing personality, thoroughness and tact, will add much to the value of the investigation and Report.

> *Sincerely yours,*
> *Richard A. Squires,*
> *Colonial Secretary.*

CHAPTER 26

The Enquiry

The Commission of Enquiry opened in Commissioner Squarey's office in the Court House in St. John's on Sept 5, 1917.

Those who appeared at 3 p.m. were Mr. Dunfield, Counsel for the International Grenfell Association, and John Grieve Esq., M.B., C.H.B., Secretary for the said Association.

Walter Baine Grieve was summoned by the Commissioner to appear at 3 p.m. and had promised to do so but did not appear. Archibald Piccott was summoned to appear before the Commissioner at 3.30 p.m. and had promised to do so, but did not appear. The Commissioner and parties present remained until 4 p.m. but the defendants did not show up. The Commissioner then issued subpoenas to W.B. Grieve, and A.W. Piccott. The Court adjourned at 4 p.m.

On September 6, the Commissioner sat at 10 a.m. Walter Baine Grieve had been subpoenaed for 10 a.m. but was not present. At 10:45, Dunfield requested Grieve be arrested if necessary, or otherwise compelled to attend and give his evidence. Just at that moment a messenger delivered the following note from Mr. Grieve:

6th Sept 1917,
To R.T. Squarey, Esq., Commissioner.
Sir:
    I am summoned by the Government to meet their

representatives at 10.45 a.m. probably you can appoint another
hour in which to take my evidence.

Your obedient servant,
(Sgd) W.B. Grieve

Dunfield said this was not a sufficient excuse and moved that
Mr. Grieve be arrested and brought in Court and required to show
why he is not present.

Judge Squarey then called Sergeant Edward Furlong, who was
present at the Court, to take the stand. After he identified himself
and took the oath, the Commissioner questioned him.

Q. You were given a subpoena by me yesterday to serve on
   Walter Baine. Grieve Esq., and also one on A.W. Piccott
   Esq., is this correct?
A. Yes.
Q. Did you serve the one on Mr. Grieve personally?
A. Yes personally on or about 5 o'clock.
Q. When did you serve the one on Mr. Piccott?
A. I served the subpoena on Mr. Piccott on or about 6 o'clock,
   personally.

Then it was Arch Piccott's turn to be sworn in and examined
by the Commissioner:

Q. Mr. Piccott, you represent the Gorton Pew Co. in
   Newfoundland?
A. At the present time, yes.
Q. Previous to this you were the Minister of Marine and
   Fisheries?
A. Yes.
Q. In your capacity of Marine and Fisheries while you were
   Minister did you ever have occasion to visit Labrador?
A. Yes.
Q. Are you aware of there being such an Institution as the
   Grenfell Association on the Labrador?

A. Yes.

Q. Have you ever visited any of the places where that Mission is established?

A. Yes.

Q. Have you ever held any conversation with the people down there immediately concerned, who may have had business relations with the Mission?

A. Yes, at Battle Harbour.

Q. Would you mind stating as near as you can recollect the conversation with them?

A. It was in 1914 or 15, I think. I was then in command of the patrol boat *Petrel*, and our port of call was Battle Harbour. One time we came in there from sea, we were short of canned goods and some other articles of food. It was the time of year when the bakeapples were ripe, and they were picking them along the coast. I went ashore to Mr. Croucher's wharf and asked him if he could let me have some bakeapples for the use of the vessel. He told me that they could not get any to buy. I left Mr. Croucher's store and went out on the wharf, when I say the wharf I mean Baine Johnston's wharf. While there I looked and saw a small rowboat crossing the harbour of Battle Harbour with two women in it. I then walked across the wharf and over towards the Grenfell store, or a place that they used to use. I presume it is their store. The reason I presume it was their store, I saw a young man by the name of Samuel Acreman whom I have known for years. I spoke to him. By this time the boat with the two women had got in by the seashore and I they had tubs in the boat filled with bakeapples. I then went down two or three steps off the wharf towards them. I discovered that there was a very young woman aboard the boat and an elderly woman who I presume was her mother. I asked them if they had the berries for sale and if they would sell them to me. The young woman felt as if she would sell the berries to me and said so. The old lady said no, she could not sell the berries. I then asked her what she was getting for the berries; she said around 35 or 40 cents per gallon. I offered her 70 cents per gallon for them. She then remarked that she was selling them to Mrs. Grieve, and would get a slip for them and later on Mrs. Grieve would go to the south side of Battle Harbour and pay them with clothes.

Q. Was Mrs. Grieve in any way connected with the Mission?

A. I could not say, it is only what she told me.

Mr. Dunfield objected as to the future intentions of Mrs. Grieve.

A. I then asked her the reason why she would not sell them to me as I wanted them for my crew. She said if I sell those berries to you then the Mission will cut me off from getting anything else from it.

Mr. Dunfield objected to the woman's reason why she should not sell the berries being given by Mr. Piccott in evidence, and suggested that the woman's name be given and her evidence be taken. Mr. Piccott said he did not know the name of the person but said she was known to Mr. Acreman, and as he recollected it, she fell in the water getting out of the boat near the shore. Captain Kennedy was there and Samuel Acreman and Mr. Piccott. They all helped her to get out of the water. Piccott continued:

During that summer I had dealings with Dr. Grieve whom I found to be a perfect gentleman, I have known Dr. Grieve for a number of years and anything I wanted from him he would give me or wanted for my crew or my ship.

Q. In your capacity as a Government official, did you ever hear of any troubles with the Customs?

A. Not officially.

Piccott was then cross examined by Dunfield:

Q. You say that is the only specific complaint that you have against the Mission?

A. That is all I have got to say.

Q. Have you any opinion you have to express either favourable or unfavourable of the work being done by the hospital Mission?

A. A man belonging to my own town by the name of French, they took him to the hospital there and treated him well, and he told me on his return, that he was treated well by Dr. Grieve and the nurses there.

And then it was the turn of W.B. Grieve who was shown a copy of the petition he'd signed and then asked by the Commissioner if he had any specific charges to make against the Mission to which he replied:

A. Yes, a very specific charge to make against them, and that is that they have departed from being a purely charitable organization and have largely developed into a mercantile concern.

Q. Can you give any proofs in support of this statement, Mr. Grieve?

A. I could by putting their late medical attendant at Battle Harbour under examination. Most of my evidence is hearsay evidence and probably not admitted in Court of Law.

Q. Have you anything further to say, Mr. Grieve?

A. I have nothing more to say than what the petition sets forth. My chief witnesses will be at Battle Harbour.

Cross examined by Dunfield:

Q. May I ask whether the petition was drafted by you or presented to you by some other person?

A. I object to answer. And I consider the question to be impertinent.

Q. If I state that the petition was drafted by you are you prepared to deny it?

A. I object to answer.

Q. You say that you have acquiesced for many years on the operation of the Grenfell Association?

A. Yes

Q. When you say you have acquiesced, what do you mean?

A. I have assisted the Mission and have been instrumental in disarming a considerable amount of opposition that was offered to it.

Q. When you say that you have acquiesced then you simply mean that you have assisted in some ways and that you have not objected to it?

A. Yes and that I have not objected to it.

Q. As to not objecting to it did you in the year 1912 write Dr. Grenfell requesting him to remove Dr. John Grieve from Battle Harbour?

A. From memory, I think I did.

Q. On what grounds?

A. Commercial interference.

Q. Could you specify the nature of such interference?

A. They departed from the cure of bodies and the cure of souls and were going into the cure of codfish, not entirely, but to some extent.

Q. Will you kindly specify what you mean by that answer?

A. Mixing themselves up with commercial business.

Q. Will you specify any definite specific instance in which Dr. Grieve associated himself?

A. I have only hearsay knowledge. I am not witness of any commercial interference.

Q. Then you wrote the letter on hearsay evidence?

A. Yes, with the full belief of the correctness of the report.

Q. Are you able to give any of your personal knowledge of any specific instance where Dr. Grieve or any other employee of the Association engaged in any commercial transaction?

A. No, not of my personal knowledge.

Q. In your next answer you say you subscribed to Section 4 of the petition.

A. Yes, I do.

Q. Which is as follows: "that on misrepresentations that this dependence of Newfoundland is largely composed of paupers the charity of the generous people of the United States has been greatly stimulated and the benefits of money and kind have been so largely increased that they have now become a menace to all other mercantile concerns on that coast who have to pay duty and freight upon the material they use or vend in the prosecution of the fisheries there." Now with regard to this paragraph, have you any personal knowledge of any instance where any employee of the Association represented to any person that this Colony is largely composed of paupers?

A. I think a matter of three or four years ago, Dr. Grieve sent a telegram which appeared in the Boston papers stating that the people on the Labrador were in a state of starvation. This was an untrue statement and Mr. Gosling, who was president of the Board of Trade that year, said representations were made to Dr. Grenfell, who was in the States, which caused him to modify the statements which had been sent from Labrador.

Q. What personal knowledge have you that that telegram was sent by Dr. Grieve?

A. It appeared in the press. He did not send it to me.

Q. Then your only knowledge of it is what you read in the newspaper report on it?

A. Yes, I did not see the original message.

Q. Are you personally in a position to say whether the contributions by people in the United States were largely increased or not?

A. I cannot say.

Q. Have you any personal knowledge, that any material given by generous people in the United States or elsewhere to the Association has been used in the prosecution of the fishery?

A. I have.

Q. Please state the instance?

A. Some four or five years ago the Grenfell Association availing of my generosity imported in my steamer bound from England to Battle Harbour 15 tons of salt or thereabouts which I carried for them freight free. I do not know whether it was used for fishery purposes or whether it was thrown away.

Q. You say you subscribed to Section 5. That Section is as follows: "That the privileges heretofore extended to the International Grenfell Association of America, successors to the Royal Mission to Deep Sea Fishermen, should either be sensibly curtailed or abolished not only on account of the above reasons but seeing that it is affiliated to certain stores trading on that coast and thereby they have an outlet for the sale of duty free merchandise introduced under the caption of goods for charitable purposes." With regard to this section, what stores do you say the Association is affiliated with?

A. To the Cape Charles cooperative stores and its branch at Battle Harbour.

Q. What connection between the stores and the Association do you intend by the word affiliation?

A. The work of inauguration was carried on by officials of the Grenfell International Instituion.

Q. Is that the only connection you have any knowledge of between the stores and the Association?

A. At the annual meeting of the Grenfell Institution in New York, Sr. Grenfell admitted that he had been mixed up with these mercantile concerns and he promised to sever his connection forewith.

Q. What official told you this?

A. That late Secretary-treasurer, Mr. Sheard, who was at the meeting.

Q. What do you mean by the phrase "mixed up?"

A. Connected with. That he had been connected with these stores.

Q. Have you any personal knowledge that these stores had sold any goods brought in duty free for charitable purposes?

A. I have.

Q. Please state the details.

A. Last year an order drawn upon my firm by my agent at Battle Harbour in favour of the Institution was questioned and upon enquiry it was found to represent goods sold, whereupon the collector of Customs made them pay duty.

Q. That refers to an order of the Association and not an order of the stores, does it not?

A. I don't know which is Association or which is cooperative stores. I think it was drawn in favour of the Association, but I could look up the order and make sure.

Q. Who was it drawn by?

A. John Croucher, my agent.

Q. Do you remember what the goods were?

A. It was an order to pay for codfish put in by Croucher. I don't know whether by the Grenfell Association or the cooperative stores.

Q. What duty free goods was the order concerned with?

A. I don't know. I know that he paid the duty here. If they had been duty paid goods he would not have paid it over again.

Q. Do you know who raised the question you speak of about the order?

A. I don't know who raised the question about the order.

Q. With regard to paragraph six of the petition, have you any definite information of this?

A. No definite information, only a belief.

Q. Have you any personal knowledge of any specific case or a breach of the law as referred to in Section 7?

A. In the matter of the duty saved on the one article to which reference has been made.

Q. You say that the Association has changed from a charitable association to a mercantile?

A. No, I don't go so far as that, but I say it is apparent to me that they are including in their duties from my standpoint a mercantile branch.

Q. When you say that they have now a mercantile branch, do you suggest that they are carrying on any commercial transactions for profit?

A. No, I do not suggest that. I mean the Directors when I say the Officials. I don't suggest that the Directors have any.

Q. Do you suggest that any of the subordinate officials, that is from the Superintendent, medical men, managers and others of the Association, do they carry on any mercantile transactions for profits?

A. I don't know what they do.

Q. Then that is equivalent to your saying you don't know any instance where they do carry on any?

A. If you press me very closely I might.

Q. Please give any specific instance you know?

A. Well, I will consider whether I will answer that question or not. It will be a very unpleasant answer if I give it.
Adjourned until the following day when Dunfield continued his examination.

Q. Will you give me an answer to my last question?

A. Under the advice of my solicitor I decline to give an answer. I make no answer.

During questioning for the rest of the day Grieve took the line that either he had no personal knowledge of events or that any evidence he would give was hearsay.

The Minister of Customs, H.W. LeMessurier, stated under oath he found nothing wrong with duties paid or not paid by the Grenfell Association. W. R. Stirling, who was in charge of Customs Inspectors, also stated he had never received any complaints.

CHAPTER 27

Harbour Grace

The Commissioner than proceeded to Harbour Grace. There, Frank McRae, Edward Parsons and James Cron were examined under oath. Neither one had much to say, but Parsons, a member of the House of Assembly who had presented the petition to the House on behalf of the fish merchants, did get some questions from the Commissioner about comments he'd made. It went like this:

Q. Did you make any remarks when you were presenting the petition in the House of Assembly?

A. Yes, I made some remarks, that is in presenting the petition, I simply said, if the report is true then it is time that the Minister of Customs should have an investigation and bring the guilty parties before the proper authorities. That is about the embodiment of my remarks, but as far as saying that I was conscious of any of the facts, I did not.

Cron said he signed the petition because he was in favour of the Grenfell Mission and it was detrimental to their work to have reports flying around about them doing crooked things, and an enquiry was the best way to get things cleared up.

The Commissioner then moved on to Carbonear where James Rorke, Robert Duff, John Udell and John Maddock were examined under oath.

Rorke said he knew nothing about what was in the petition. Duff said he agreed to sign the petition for the purposes of getting an enquiry. Udell appeared on behalf of his father, who had signed the petition, and had very little to say either for or against the Mission.

John Maddock, representing the firm of J. and J. Maddock, said he had traded on the French Shore and in Labrador for a total of thirty summers, including five years before the Mission came, and sold thousands of dollars worth of goods. He said his sales dropped about 50 per cent after the Mission arrived and a year or so later dropped down to about 30 per cent. Business was particularly bad at St. Anthony and people said they were getting their shop goods from the Mission. He had no knowledge of how business was done at the Mission and said the petition had been signed simply because the sale of his shop goods fell off when the Mission arrived and "injured a man's business considerably."

CHAPTER 28

St. Anthony and the Story of Kirky

T he Commissioner proceeded to St. Anthony where those examined included Joseph Moore and Frederick Ollerhead, as well as Noah Simms, sub-collector of Customs, and relieving officer Luke Biles and Wilfred Grenfell.

Examination of Wilfred T. Grenfell, taken on oath at St. Anthony the 19th day of September A. D. 1917. Examination was by Mr. Hunt.

Q. You have been on this coast a considerable amount of time, Doctor, I think?

A. Yes, twenty-six years.

Q. Why did you first visit it?

A. I was asked to do so by Sir Francis Hopwood during the winter of 1892.

Q. Why did he want you to come?

A. He thought we should reduplicate among the fishermen on he Newfoundland Grand Banks the work that we had been doing in the North Sea.

Q. When you first came here did you have any assistants with you?

A. Yes, I had a private secretary.

Q. Where were your first headquarters?

A. At that time? I did not have any. I sailed back again that same year.

Q. Did you come here in a Mission vessel?

A. Yes, in a schooner.

Q. What work did you do the first year?
A. Only God knows what we did the first year we came here.

Dr. Grenfell paused and looked at his hands and then at the floor after saying those words. He seemed lost in thought for a moment but then proceeded. "We just cruised around the coast doing hospital work in every nook and cranny. We also did a lot of charitable work."

Q. What did you mean, Doctor, when you said only God knows what you did?' Can you give us an example of some incident that you ran into, or what the medical condition was like at that time?"

Dr. Grenfell once again paused and cleared his throat before continuing. "Sometimes, Your Honour, you don't even like to be reminded of certain incidents that you encountered, but since you asked for an example I can certainly give you one," he said. And for the next half hour or so, he held everyone spellbound as he related the following story:

"It was a bitter cold morning during the first week of January 1901 at Winter House Cove, a small place about three miles inland from Rigolet in Northern Labrador and populated by just one family. Emo Jeffery was a young married half Inuit with two children. He lived all winter in this small cove and spent most of his time trapping along his ten mile trap line.

Emo was a strong, powerful man, more than six feet tall. His now deceased father was a native of Scotland who had come to Labrador as a young man on a ship bringing supplies for the Hudson Bay Company and the Moravian Mission and had stayed on to marry an Inuit woman. He never returned to Scotland. Emo had his father's height and red hair but looked like his mother. He had married an Inuit woman from further north and brought her to live in Rigolet where he had fished with his father in the summer.

On this bitterly cold morning in Winter Horse Cove as Emo arose from his feather bed and walked out into the small kitchen he felt the warmth from the wood stove that he had been stoking all night. He put water in the iron kettle and set it on the stove to boil as he prepared his breakfast.

On this particular morning Emo was going to his trap line for a two-night stay that would take him far inland. The night before, he'd found his wife was coming down with the flu; she had a high temperature and was coughing nonstop. However, his traps had to be attended to above all cost; he needed fur if he was to get food at the Hudson Bay Store to stay alive.

Emo deeply loved his wife and two daughters, especially the youngest, Kirkina, a lively child of three whom he called "my little Kirky."

Emo had prayed she would be a boy, but when the midwife delivered another girl and he set his eyes on little Kirky, he immediately forgot his hopes for a son.

Now, getting ready for his trip, he very carefully wrapped the bannock that his wife had prepared for him the night before in a piece of cloth and put it in his seal skin packsack, along with a chunk of seal fat in a screw cap bottle. Out in the wilds, he would eat the bannock and use the seal fat as grease to fry the wild meat he caught in his traps.

He filled the stove with firewood and then, with his snowshoes strapped to his sealskin boots, he blew out the candle and was far from his house long before dawn made its first streak across the starry sky.

It is almost impossible to describe the meager construction that went into log huts like Emo's during this period and it was simply because people lacked proper tools and couldn't afford anything better.

Emo's hut was built of round logs cut and shaped with an axe. The seams in the wall were corked with moss on the inside and clay on the outside. Emo had put a wooden floor in half the cabin; the rest had a mud floor baked hard with heat from the homemade stove. In each end of the cabin there was a small window close to the roof.

Emo was proud of his winter cabin; at least he wasn't living in a caribou skin tent like most of his relatives. And he was glad to be close to the Hudson Bay store at Rigolet. As long as he caught fur to make a little money he and his family would not starve during the winter.

Now, picture little three-year-old Kirky, waking up on a bitterly cold frosty morning and wanting to pee and feeling hungry. She woke to find her daddy gone and the house cold and empty. She got out of bed and walked along the rough wooden floor then stepped down onto the hard black mud floor that was so cold her little feet almost stuck on. Looking around in the semi-darkness she saw her sealskin boots near the table and reached out to quickly put them on. Frost stung her feet, but she ignored the cold and hungrily ran to the table where she saw some bannock left from her father's breakfast. It had frozen but she gobbled it down anyway. It was then she peed herself. The warm pee ran down her legs and into her skin boots.

"Oh my," she told people when interviewed in later years, "the pee felt so warm I couldn't stop until I had it all done." Minutes later she was standing in icy cold urine and with that she ran for her bed.

Shortly after Emo left, his wife, Polly, got into a terrible fit of coughing, so much so that she thought she would lose her breath. The coughing woke the oldest child who immediately got out of the bed she shared with her sister and into her mother's bed. That left Kirky alone in a bed huddled close to the icy logs that made up the outer wall. (Anyone knowing anything about those log tilts that were scattered around the wilderness deep in the bays of Newfoundland and Labrador knows they were no place to have children during the winter unless someone was prepared to keep a fire burning night and day. Children had to sleep together to keep each other warm.)

In this particular case, Polly fell asleep after her coughing fit. In less than an hour, with no one stoking the fire, the log tilt was the same as a deep freeze. Kirky got into her icy bed wearing her wet skin boots and even with the blankets pulled over her head she couldn't get warm. In telling this story afterwards, she said that she began crying because of the pain from her wet, cold feet.

"Momma, Momma," she sobbed but her mother didn't hear her. In a few minutes her feet became numb and pain free and she fell asleep. It is not known how long she slept before she awoke, screaming loudly. Polly jumped out of bed and held the shivering child in her arms. As she tucked the little girl into her bed with her sister she wondered why she had her boots on. Her heart sank as she saw that the boots were two chunks of solid ice and little Kirky's feet were frozen blocks.

Polly knew her young daughter was in trouble. Frozen feet could kill her. With Kirky in her arms, screaming and holding her tight, she ran into the kitchen where she sat her on a chair next to the cold stove. Polly put kindling into the stove, lit the fire, and pulled the chair closer. She knew she had to get the skin boots off Kirky's feet as quickly as possible.

When she felt a little heat from the stove, Polly put Kirky on the table and tried to pull the boots off but to no avail. The boots were frozen solid to the little girl's feet and legs. Polly moved the table closer to the stove and let the child's feet hang out over the edge.

This Inuit woman was not stupid. She had lived all her life in the wilds of Labrador and had seen almost everything when it came to medical problems. But this was something she'd never dreamt possible, especially in her own home.

Knowing what she had to do to get the boots off, she quickly put the kettle on the stove, noticing that the water in it had frozen and would have to melt before it got hot. As she waited for the water to warm, she held Kirky's frozen feet inside her nightdress. When the water was hot she put the little girl back on the table. She soaked a towel in the kettle and wrapped it around the skin boots until they grew slack on Kirky's feet.

"The boots will have to be cut off," she said to herself as she took a cobbler's knife from the shelf over the stove and, with tears in her eyes, started to cut into the boots. Kirky screamed with pain and almost went into convulsions as she held her down with one hand and cut the boots off with the other. Soon the boots were off, revealing frozen legs and feet. The stench of urine told Polly that Kirky had peed in her boots, causing the boots as well as her feet and legs to freeze solid.

Fearing for her daughter's survival, Polly tried to think of a remedy the old folks used for frost burns. She couldn't remember anyone being treated for anything as severe as this. As she looked at her daughter's legs and feet she could see blisters forming, huge bladders were ballooning all over. In utter desperation and agony she started crying as her screaming, wide-eyed daughter clung to her.

I suppose it will never be known, and one's imagination could never comprehend how this young Inuit mother felt on that cold windswept morning, huddled around a home made stove and standing on a mud floor in a log cabin with a minus 40 degree temperature outside. As tears fell from her eyes, she knew the old fashioned remedies weren't enough. It would take a miracle to save her child's life.

Polly kept her daughter wrapped in a woolen blanket for most of the morning and wept as the little girl cried with pain. Just before noon, she looked at Kirky's legs and her heart sank when she saw the child's legs were a mass of blisters. It looked as though there was one large blister extending from the bottom of her feet to about two inches from her knees, the height of the skin boots. The blisters were so large that Kirky's legs and feet were twice their normal size.

"Mommy is going to have to let the water out of the blisters," she said as her daughter stared at her, not knowing or understanding what she meant. Polly took a large sewing needle and with unsteady fingers let the water out of the blisters and watched it run out onto the table. Kirkina screamed in pain as her mother tried to do something for her.

Although she may not have known it, one thing Polly did right was to give Kirky plenty of water to drink. This prevented her system from completely drying out because of the fluids leaking from her feet and legs. Although she had nothing to give her daughter for pain and no one to turn to for help, Polly kept the stove full of wood and the cabin warm. She had one thing going for her; there was lots of firewood stacked in the porch at the entrance of the house.

Polly made up a bed for Kirky on the table so that she could keep an eye on her. During the afternoon she examined her daughter's feet again and saw that the nails on all of her toes were completely lifted off by the watery blisters that covered them. It seemed that every time she looked at Kirkina's feet and legs she saw something happening that was a little worse than before.

As the sun began to set and the long Labrador night began to close in on them, the child began crying again and calling out to her father.

"Daddy, Daddy, I want my Daddy," she said as her mother tried to comfort her by saying her daddy would soon be home. Polly was struck by the agonizing thought that Emo was gone for at least two nights and would Kirky still be alive when he got back? She thought about what he would say to her when he returned and found his little girl in such a deplorable condition. Polly was so frightened she felt like running away. Yes, running out into the cold frosty night and dying. But this mother could not leave her children come what may. It was then that Polly put her hands over her face and wept in agony.

All night, the desperate mother sat in her homemade rocking chair near the roaring stove with her suffering child across her knees, trying to console her in a way that would somehow ease her pain. But it was to no avail, the child cried and groaned all night. As the dawn broke and the sun came up, Polly knew it was a rough day ahead for the child and her.

Her older daughter, who was four, sat silently on a wooden bench close to the stove, looking at her mother and knowing there was something terribly wrong with her young sister. Keeping Kirky wrapped in a heavy woolen blanket, Polly gently sat her on a couch near the stove and, after a severe bout of coughing, she went to the little pantry and brought out a cloth bag full of rolled oats.

"Mom is going to make a dipper full of porridge for your breakfast, my dears," she said in a voice loud enough for the two children to hear. Polly was glad to see Kirky eat a bowl of porridge and shortly afterwards fall asleep.

Polly herself was still feeling ill. She was also very worried about what Eno's reaction would be when he returned and saw Kirky. She was sure that he would go out of his mind and blame her for not looking after the child.

The first day after leaving home, Emo spent most of his time tending his traps close to the river. Finding they were frozen from the severe frost that had gripped the whole of Labrador, he had to work to get them back in working order and this took more time than he had anticipated. When he got to his trapping tilt it was almost dark and he realized he would have to spend two nights there because it would take him a full day to look at his traps further to the west and in the country. When he had the fire going, he took flour and baking powder and made enough flapjacks for two days. That would keep him well fed till he got back home.

Emo's little trapping tilt was six hours walk from Winter House Cove. The next day, after checking his traps to the westward, he started walking back to the tilt with plans to bring in extra firewood for the cold night ahead. When he arrived it was three in the afternoon and the sun was low in the western sky. He lit the fire, put the kettle on the stove, and made tea. In telling the story afterwards, he said he was sure he heard a voice telling him something was wrong and he had better go home. At first he tried to shrug it off, but the feeling made him so uneasy that he decided to pack up and head for home. He knew it would be hard walking in the dark and hauling his heavy load of furs but, be that as it may, Emo put on his snowshoes and headed out on his six hour trek for his home in Winter House Cove.

Kirkina slept for about two hours. When she awoke, she started screaming and calling for her father. Polly tried to console her, but the child acted as though she were going into convulsions. Bringing Kirky to the table, Polly took the blanket off her and looked at her legs and feet. What she saw frightened her so much she felt sick to her stomach.

The flesh was literally hanging from the little girl's bones and her legs were swollen three times their normal size. Polly looked in horror, knowing there was nothing she could do for her child, only look at her and watch her die.

"If she was only South where the Grenfell doctors were maybe they could cure her or at least give her something for her pain," she whispered to herself as she wished for the hundredth time that Emo was there. But he was many miles away in the wilds of Labrador. There was no way to reach him. He'd said he would be gone for at least two nights.

Looking more closely at Kirky, she saw there were red streaks going up the child's upper legs. She knew there was no doubt about it. The child was in severe pain and only the mercy of God would save her.

Meanwhile, Emo was trudging along through the snow, following the snowshoe track he had made two days earlier. Although it was night, there was enough light from the stars and the northern lights for him to see where he was going. He stopped at a place about halfway on his journey and ate some of the venison that he had cooked earlier in the day along with a little bannock. This gave him strength as he pressed forward on his journey.

As dark settled in on the little log cabin, Polly prepared for the night. She brought in more wood and stacked it near the stove. She knew this would be a really cold night, and it was much better to have the wood within reach because the fire would have to be kept burning till Emo returned. She cooked a pot full of pork and beans for supper and was happily surprised when Kirkina ate a plate full. She was encouraged all the more when the child stopped crying for a while. Taking her into her arms, she sang her and her sister an Inuit lullaby.

"Your daddy will be here after a while, my dears," she would say, little knowing that Emo was racing toward home with a strange feeling deep in his heart that all was not right.

Polly sat rocking her daughter in the light of a tin kerosene lamp that a relative had sent from Scotland. It was one of Emo's prized possessions. The light was much better then the seal oil lights that most everyone used at the time.

As Polly sat in the glow of the orange flickering lamp light with her dying child in her arms, she thought about the struggle it was to make a living in the wilds of Labrador.

There was nothing in the way of Government help in supplying medical assistance. She had heard about Dr. Grenfell and the Medical Mission that came around in the summer. But in the fall or winter if anyone got sick or had an accident they had to go back to relying on the homemade remedies as their forefathers did for generations, or die.

Polly had endured many problems in her short lifetime. She had given birth to two children at home with no medical help whatsoever. She had seen people die of all kinds of diseases and accidents. Neglect was prevalent everywhere. As she sat there burdened in sorrow, she wondered if she should run away from it all and never come back. But where could she go? She felt like a trapped animal, there was nowhere to run. The truth was she loved her children and Emo too much to leave. However, when she thought about what Emo would do or say to her when he saw little Kirkina, it made her cringe in fear. But above it all she held her child tightly in her arms, praying that things would turn out all right.

As Emo drew closer to his house, he could smell the smoke from the stovepipe and in just a few minutes he could see the light through the window above the snowdrift. When he got within a hundred feet of the cabin he stopped and called, "Hello, Hello."

Polly had just finished putting wood in the stove and was again seated in the rocking chair with Kirky in her arms when she thought she heard someone calling. She stopped rocking and sat up straight. Maybe it was her imagination, but she was sure someone had called out.

Emo saw no movement in the house and called again, "Polly, hey Polly."

Whenever he was away from the house for an overnight trip he would always call to her before he entered the door. She would open the door and put her arms around him and hug him. Now, he waited a few seconds for the door to open and when it didn't he took off his packsack and snowshoes and left them outside before pulling on the string and lifting the door latch. Stepping inside, he sensed something wrong. Then he saw his wife sitting in the rocking chair holding Kirkina.

Emo's beard and eyebrows were covered in icicles, and his clothes looked as if they were frozen to his body.

"My good lord, Polly, is there something wrong with Kirky?" he asked as his wife burst into tears. She could not speak.

With difficulty, Emo took off his frozen sealskin mitts and rushed to her side demanding an answer. "Polly what's wrong?" he said, knowing there was something terribly wrong with his daughter.

"Her feet and legs are frozen, Emo," Polly managed to get out between the sobs and the crying. Emo said afterwards that was the worst statement he'd ever heard.

"Legs and feet frozen," he yelled back as Kirky opened her eyes wide and stared at her father. "Daddy, Daddy," she cried.

Emo tore off his jacket and tore the icicles from his face as he rushed to Polly and took the little girl from her. He could smell the stench of rotting flesh and his face paled as Kirky screamed in agony.

"Polly, what happened? What happened, Polly?" he asked as he put his daughter across his knees.

Kirkina put her arms around her father's neck as he put her on the table and slowly removed the blanket wrapping her. What he saw made his heart sink to the bottom of his boots. "Oh my God, Kirkina is finished," were the words that echoed through his head. He wanted to yell but his father had taught him never to panic, to always remain calm no matter what happened. "You're going to be alright, Kirky. You're going to be alright," he said to his daughter, being careful not to frighten her any more than she was already. "But dear God," his inner voice told him, "Kirkina is finished."

Emo knew there wasn't much use in trying to get an explanation from his wife about what had happened to his daughter; it might frighten the child all the more if she heard them talking about it. Right now, he only wanted to find out if there was anything that could be done to save her life.

He knew there was no kind of medicine in the world that could cure the child's feet and legs, but what could he do? He wasn't a doctor. He was fully aware that the only doctors or nurses available were at Battle Harbour in the south and the Moravian hospital many miles to the north. But he wondered if there was anything at the Hudson Bay store in Rigolet that he could get that would ease Kirky's pain. Emo took his beloved little girl up into his arms again and held her tight. He was broken hearted knowing there was nothing he could do.

Emo hid his tears and tried to make his little girl comfortable. He knew that was about the only thing he could do at the moment. After he rocked the child for a few minutes, she fell off to sleep.

Emo became very angry. He looked at his wife with blazing eyes and asked, "What happened, Polly? What happened to Kirky? Why did you let her go out into the cold and freeze?" His wife stood near the window, to frightened to answer. "In the name of God, what happened to my baby?" Emo demanded. Polly finally got up enough courage to answer. "She never went out in the cold, Emo," she said as her husband looked at her with a puzzled look and asked again, "Then what happened?"

Trying to be calm, Polly told him what she thought had happened. Kirky had got up after her father left to get something to eat and then put on her skin boots and peed in them. Polly said she was sick and asleep but woke up when she heard Kirky crying. By then it was too late, her legs and feet were frozen solid. Emo could see his wife was just as broken hearted as he was and realized this was no time to argue. Something had to be done to save Kirky's life. Arguing would only make the problem worse.

"Did you put anything on her legs, Polly?" he asked.

"No," she replied. "There's nothing here that I could put on them."

Emo looked at his wife and saw that she was at her wit's end and about to collapse. He went over to her and put his arms around her and the two of them cried.

Polly finally fell asleep. Emo looked again at his daughter's legs and feet and seeing the state they were in he knew there was no possible way she could survive without losing them. The thought made him sick because he knew there was no medical assistance nearby, let alone a hospital where amputations could be preformed. The grieving father cried and groaned all night. Just before dawn, he made breakfast for his family, having decided he would take Kirky to Rigolet to see if anyone there could offer suggestions on how to help.

When Polly commented on how bad the weather was Emo said that made no difference, they were taking Kirky to Rigolet to see if something could be done for her there.

When the sun came up and the wind dropped, he told Polly to get Kirkina ready for the three mile trip to Rigolet. He said they would put her and her sister in a box on the sleigh and haul them there. When he had his sealskin parka and mitts on, Emo went outside to get his sleigh ready. The trip to Rigolet took about an hour with Emo out front hauling the sleigh and Polly, wearing snowshoes, pushing in the rear.

They arrived at the Hudson Bay store and Emo went quickly inside. The manager, James Wilson, was a very gentle man Emo knew well; after Emo briefly told him what had happened he told him to bring Kirky in.

Emo went outside and lifted the oldest child out of the box and Polly carried her into the store. Emo then opened the store door wide and hauled the sleigh and Kirkina inside.

There were seven or eight people in the store and they had all heard Emo's conversation with James Wilson. Emo warned everyone that the child's feet and legs were not a very pretty sight before he unwrapped them.

Gently taking Kirkina out of the box, he placed her on the counter. Everyone's eyes were on her, not knowing what to expect. As Emo took away the heavy blankets, you could smell the decaying flesh. When he showed the people her legs and feet, there was quite a stir among them.

Emo looked at the reaction of each person as they stared in disbelief at the child. Some only glanced and turned away, while others quietly commented that the poor child was finished. One man said, "If only you could get her to the Hospital at Battle Harbour, you might be able to save her life."

Emo then turned to the store manager and asked if he had any medicine to help his daughter. Wilson said the only thing he had in the form of medicine was Aspirin tablets and that was the only kind of medicine he would find in all of Rigolet.

Everyone knew there was no hope for this little girl. There was only one thing her father could do and that was just try and keep her comfortable until she died.

Knowing there was no use in staying at the store, Emo told Polly to get the child ready for the return trip back home.

James Wilson wanted Emo and his family to stay at Rigolet. He said they could stay at his house. Emo thanked him for the offer but said they were going home. When he asked if he could have some Aspirins, Wilson gave him his last container of twelve.

Emo thanked him, then put the dying child back into the sleigh and headed back to his log cabin. It was now afternoon. As they trudged sadly home, Emo decided he would not let his beloved Kirky die without a fight.

In the log cabin, he got the fire going and put the kettle on to boil. He asked Polly to cook porridge for a meal, saying he needed a full stomach to carry out what he had planned to do. Polly did not understand what he was trying to say to her. She looked at him but said nothing.

He rocked Kirky while the porridge cooked. After she was fed he gave her an Aspirin. Polly and the eldest daughter ate but before Emo had a chance to get to the table, Kirky was asleep. He gently laid her on his and Polly's bed.

When he'd finished eating his porridge and the dishes were washed and put away he told Polly to put the older girl to bed. When they were alone he told his wife what he was going to do.

"There is no chance that Kirky will live another twenty- four hours in the condition she is in right now," he said as he pointed out how fast the infection was setting in, something made clear by the red streaks going up the child's thighs and the fever that had started.

"Sit down, Polly, and I will tell you what I am going to do to save Kirky's life," he said as Polly listened with her face in her hands. "Polly," he said slowly, "there is only one thing left to save Kirky's life and that is to cut off her legs. Her legs and feet are nothing but rotten flesh and it's only a matter of hours before gangrene sets in, then it will be too late."

Polly sat silently, wiping the tears from her eyes.

"We have a choice, Polly. We either remove her infected legs or watch her die a horrible death."

"I can't do it Emo. I can't even stand to hear you talk about it, let alone help you do it."

"Polly, if we want to try and save Kirky's life we have to remove her two legs right away. If we put it off till tomorrow we may have to cut them off right up to her thighs."

"My God, Emo, the shock will kill her."

"Doctors in hospitals do it all the time to save lives," said Emo. He knew he had to convince his wife to help him, he couldn't do it alone. "Listen," he said in as calm a voice as he could, "her legs will have to come off at the knee joints. You will hold her down on the table. I will tie a tight string around her leg just above the knee to prevent any bleeding, then I will chop the leg off with the axe. It will be so quick she won't feel any pain." Polly was speechless, she felt as though her tongue was stuck to the roof of her mouth. Emo continued, "We will have two woolen socks filled with flour ready to pull up over her legs. This will stop the bleeding when I release the string I'll put on before I cut the legs off. We will press the flour tight against the severed area."

After a lot of talking and persuading, Emo convinced his wife to help him carry out this heart wrenching act.

Emo had some tools his father had left him, including a stainless steel axe used for trimming boat planks. This is what he would use to cut off his child's legs. He filled a pot with water and put it on the stove to boil. He would use the water to sterilize the axe. Deep down in his heart he had a sick feeling as he prepared himself for the awful task ahead.

He told Polly to get a pair of new woolen stockings and half fill them with white flour. He went to the shed to get his axe. It was already very sharp but not quite to his liking so he took a small whetstone and touched up the edge. When he was satisfied the axe was sharp enough he carried it into the house.

We will never know what really went on that evening, or the details of the axe amputation of Kirkina's legs.

We do know that Emo and Polly put a piece of heavy wood under the legs near the child's knee joints and used a heavy wooden mallet to strike the axe.

They laid the child on her back and tied her to the table. Kirky was crying loudly, not knowing what was going to happen. Her father told her that he was going to make her better. "It will hurt you first, Kirky, but only for a little while then you will be better," he reassured her.

The desperate parents put a cloth over their daughter's eyes and tied it tight around the back of her head to prevent her from seeing what was happening.

Emo took a piece of fishing line and tied it tightly above her two knees with a slip knot. The knot would easily come untied when he or Polly tugged on one end after the flour socks were in place, and the flour had hopefully stopped the bleeding. When everything was ready, Polly put her head close to Kirky's and hugged her. She heard the thud of the axe as it severed the first leg. She thought she felt the pain herself.

It was only a matter of seconds and another thud of the axe and Kirkina's two legs were off. Emo used his cobbler's needle to close the skin over the stumps of her severed legs. He then quickly pulled the two socks full of flour up and over the stumps and secured them. He waited for a few minutes and removed the fishing line, hoping she would not lose too much blood. He rolled the severed legs in a towel and took them outside to dispose of them.

He and Polly lifted Kirky off the table and gently placed her on their bed. Shortly afterwards, Emo looked and saw there was no bleeding around the wounds, it appeared everything was okay.

In less then an hour, the child's crying ceased and she never cried again about pain caused by the amputation of her two legs.

During that night Emo and Polly took turns keeping the fire going and closely watching the child to see if her condition changed. In the morning, they were delighted when Kirkina wanted her breakfast. Within a month, her wounds were completely healed and she was going around the floor just like any other child. Her father also hauled her around on a sleigh, even taking a trip to Rigolet.

The next spring, Emo and his family were back in Rigolet. When I arrived on a medical trip along the Labrador Coast. Usually, I would tie up to the main wharf and after word got around I would start doing the medical clinic aboard the boat. If anyone was too sick to come to the boat, I would visit them in their home. On this particular trip, Kirkina was the talk of the town. The manager of the Hudson Bay store told me what had happened with her legs and I could hardly believe what I was hearing. I was stunned to hear such a terrible story.

I went back aboard my boat and told my crew I had an urgent call ashore and would be back in an hour. I took my medical bag and walked to the house where the manager had told me Emo lived.

"Are you Emo Jeffery?" I asked when a tall, red haired man came to the door.

"Yes, Dr. Grenfell, I am," he answered.

"Can I come in?" I asked.

"Yes, you certainly can," he said.

I stepped into the neat little house, put down my medical bag and Emo introduced me to his wife.

"I heard that you had to amputate your child's legs last winter in order to save her life?" I said to the two of them.

Emo spoke up, his wife kept silent. "Yes, I did, Doctor. In fact, I cut off both of her legs. If I hadn't done it we were sure that she would have died in less then two days."

Emo told me the whole story and I could hardly believe my ears.

"Where is the child now?" I asked.

"I've made a pair of wooden legs and feet for her, and she is playing in the other room. Would you like to see her?" he asked.

"Yes, please," I said.

Emo called out to Kirky saying someone wanted to see her. I sat there not knowing what to expect as I watched the latch on the bedroom door lift up and slowly open."

"It was here that I got the biggest shock of my entire life," Dr. Grenfell told BBC Radio in an interview years later. "A little three-year-old girl with her two legs missing up to her knees entered the room. She was wearing homemade wooden clogs that thumped the floor as she scuffed along. In one hand she had a short birch walking stick, and in the other she carried a gallon paint can that dragged the floor with each step. In the can was a big-eyed rag doll that had one arm hanging out over the edge. The little girl looked at me and gave me the most beautiful smile I had ever seen."

"This is Doctor Grenfell, Kirky," said Emo.

"Hello, Doctor," she said. It was too much for me. I had never seen or heard of anything like this before. I turned and put my hands to my face and cried.

After telling the story, Dr. Grenfell once again started crying and wiping tears from his eyes. Judge Squarey too was moved to tears as he motioned Grenfell to continue:

"The next day, we left Rigolet with the little girl and I will never forget the farewell between Emo Jeffrey and his daughter. The father was broken-hearted, but he figured it was the best thing for his legless child. I brought the youngster to St. Anthony and she went to school there for a year. But a friend of mine heard about her and offered to pay her fare and bring her to Boston where she had legs of the finest quality made to fit her. She was there for four or five years going to school, finally she wanted to go back home.

She always talked about how she wanted to see her father and family. She came back to St. Anthony and stayed for a while but wanted to go home to Rigolet. We did not how to break the news that her father had died in a drowning accident five years earlier. Our staff got her ready and put her on the mail steamer going north accompanied by one of our nurses. On the way back the nurse told her about her father. She was so devastated by the news that she took her two artificial legs and threw them away over the side of the boat.

She spent the rest of the year with her family. The next summer, we brought her back to St. Anthony and sent her to England to have new legs made and continue her education. We had word from her last month that she is now in training to be a nurse, specializing in midwifery. Our plan is to send her back to Rigolet as a trained midwife for that area."

CHAPTER 29

Heart Breaking Labrador Story

W hen Dr. Grenfell had finished speaking, Judge Squarey adjourned the court for the day. He advised everyone that court would resume at 9 a.m. the following day. The next morning, there was a full house when Dr. Grenfell was called to the stand.

Judge Squarey began by saying, "The last question I asked you was about the work you did the first year you came. However, after the moving story you related to this court about the young child at Rigolet we felt we could not continue without having time to think about it first. I will include that information as part of your testimony, Doctor. However we are now back in court and will proceed with the enquiry."

Q. After the first year you said you went back to England, is this correct?

A. Yes, I went to St. John's on the way back handed my report to the Governor, the leaders of the government and the opposition.

Q. And then went back to England?

A. Yes.

Q. Did you come back again?

A. Yes, in the spring. I had no headquarters. I sailed all over the place again.

Q. When did you first establish your headquarters?

A. It was a long time ago. I have a history of it all. I built the hospital in 1893; I brought back two doctors and nurses with me. Then in the fall I paid them all off and went back to England. The only reason that I came back was that the Governor and the leaders of both Houses wrote to the Society saying they would erect two hospitals if we would run them. It was on the distinct understanding that no charges whatsoever would be made on anything we brought in that we agreed to consider the matter.

Q. You built a hospital at St. Anthony that year then went back home again to England?

A. Yes.

Q. Did you come out the next year?

A. Yes, I came out again.

Q. And of course your work increased from year to year?

A. Oh yes. I went home that third year, I remember, and the forth year I went to Iceland. The fifth year I came back again. That would be in 1897, wouldn't it? Well I'm not quite sure that I stayed at St. Anthony that year. Oh yes, that was the first winter that I stayed here, the first winter that I put up upon the coast. Yes, I spent that winter here. I hired rooms.

Q. Up to that time had you obtained the service of any assistants?

A. Yes.

Q. All of those who assisted you were under your instructions?

A. Yes.

Q. Was there anyone with you paid by the government?

A. No. There was the distinct stipulation that there would be no control outside of the board and myself. I made all arrangements with the government by correspondence. I have copies of the minutes of council in a book called "The Harvest of the Sea."

Q. Could you give us a short outline of the work at the present time?

A. Well, there are five hospitals and two cottage hospitals, if you care to dignify Pilley's Island with the name.
We also have a large hospital ship and a small cottage

hospital at Spotted Islands that we operate during the summer. There is the Seaman's Institute at St. John's, the school here, the orphanage, a machine shop, the industrial school, the agricultural department and the sawmill and farm at Roddickton. There is also the hospital steamer and four or five motorboats, which we operate to get into small areas.

Q. Have you read the petition to the House of Assembly?

A. Yes.

Q. The first part of that deals with the fact that 'on misrepresentation that this dependency of Newfoundland is largely composed of paupers' and so on. Is this true, you have collected money in foreign countries? Can you answer that?

A. I have written altogether about fourteen books. For twenty years I have been writing for magazines. If in these writings of mine they can find anything to that effect, I do not know of it.

I am prepared to stand by what I have written. I lecture on and off. I am going to lecture again this winter on my work in this country. This allegation in the petition is absolutely ridiculous.

Q. Then the charity "of the generous people of the United States has not been greatly stimulated and the benefits in money and kind been so largely increased that they have become a menace to all other mercantile concerns upon the coast" owing to misrepresentations made by you.

A. I am not conscious of making any misrepresentations. I merely state my views and opinions, by which I am prepared to stand. I also claim that I know more then most people about the life and conditions down here.

Q. Has anything ever been entered that you are aware of that has been sold for profit by the association?

A. What do you mean?

Q. The charge infers that you obtained from the generous people in the United States goods that have been entered duty free here and which have been sold to the disadvantage of other mercantile firms?

A. That was done on one occasion at Spotted Islands. That is a place run by the Y.M.C.A. of the College of Physicians and Surgeons of New York where one of the young men sold some of the clothes he had brought down to enable him to help erect and add to the dispensary. I wrote about it to Mr. LeMessurier and paid the duties. He had all the letters about it.

Q. You yourself brought it to the notice of the Customs?

A. Yes, certainly. Mistakes must occur occasionally in so large a work as ours – thus, two of our doctors married without licenses once. They didn't know they needed a license to marry here.

Q. Does your Mission interfere with trade at all?

A. I would not say that it interferes. I would say assisted, and most certainly, not as a Mission. But the dissemination of information among the people certainly changes the conditions of trade. The idea of the cooperative stores is to improve the methods of doing business. I personally founded the cash stores. I think that I founded them all.

Q. What was your motive?

A. Chiefly to help the people to a living diet. It was useless treating patient's whose trouble more then half came from dietetic deficiencies, as they were getting nothing but dry diet.

I helped to found two cooperative stores in London before I saw this country. I took three starving children home to England with me in the schooner, during the first three years I was here.

Q. Are your stores capitalized by American business people?

A. Not one cent that I know of. There was some American money loaned to the Cape Charles cooperative store. Some of the volunteer students of Battle Harbour took shares last summer, I understood they bought these themselves, and one friend lent $500 at interest to this store.

Q. Do they invest without receiving dividends or interest?

A. No.

Q. Is it correct that Americans capitalize these stores?

A. No. I remember telling Mr. Baine Grieve a couple of years ago that American businessmen were more than willing to give me the money if I wanted it. I did not tell him I had the money because I did not have it.

Q. Do you know of any instances where the Customs authorities have detected breaches of the law?

A. No, they never did. My own auditors discovered the Karnopp matter. It was a case where goods were stolen or sold by the Mission and the accounts subsequently falsified. Goods were bought from Pittman and Shaw in the usual way, he bought more then he needed and embezzled the money. The goods were imported free of duty.

Q. Is there no case where the Customs compelled the payment of duty on goods?

A. No, there is no case.

Q. And as regards to this petition, there is nothing in it?

A. No, it is a series of statements with absolutely nothing in them.

Q. Have you read the counter petition filed by Mr. Watson?

A. Yes.

Q. Is it correct in every particular?

A. Yes. In reference to #9, I may say that it was distinctly understood by the Government of Newfoundland and us when I came here that we were not to pay duty on anything we had come into this country because we had to raise the money to buy all these things. It was hard to raise the money and guarantee an income. It was in our minds to ask for a Government inspection but as the war was on we thought it wasn't a good time. That was last year, I think. The matter was discussed by the directors and is shown in their minutes.

Q. With regard to these cooperative stores, how many are there?

A. There's one at St. Anthony (headquarters), Brahat, Flowers Cove, Red Bay, Cape Charles, Englee and Forteau.

Q. Are they separate from the Mission?

A. Yes, absolutely.

Dr. Grenfell gave a complete rundown of the cooperative business around the Northern Peninsula and along the Labrador Coast. He told the Commission he could not understand the mentality of the floating fish merchants out of St. John's.

"If those merchants wanted," he said, "they could become suppliers for the cooperative stores instead of their enemy, and they could benefit greatly from this. For instance, they could send their schooners to the coast with a load of goods for the cooperative stores and take back a load of salted fish to the market for the co-op and even deliver it to foreign countries, getting cash for everything they did. I told this to Mr. Walter Grieve one day while we were having lunch at Battle Harbour. But no, all they wanted was to be able to control the complete codfishery along the coast of Labrador. It made no difference whether they made money, broke even, or went in the hole. I tried to explain to some of them about all the new cash we were spending in the different places where we were operating, and the new markets that we had, especially in the United States, but it was no use, they were only set on getting revenge. And when this enquiry is complete, Your Honour, you will find out that they don't even know what they are trying to get revenge for."

Q. You said earlier something about people not getting proper food to help them fight off disease, could you elaborate somewhat on this, or do you know of any such incidents, or have any examples to give?

A. Yes, there are many examples of people dying of starvation and not far from stores with food in them.

Q. Did any of these incidents occur since you came here?

A. Yes, I have them here in my medical notes.
Q. Could you give us one example?
A. Yes, Your Honour.

Grenfell then went on to tell the following tale:

"One fall, I was way up north on the Labrador Coast helping to combat a terrible outbreak of typhoid fever. People were dying almost every day, especially young children. We knew we had delayed our departure for too long. The ground was covered with snow and it was freezing over so we had no other choice but to pack our bags and leave immediately or stay there till next July.

In order to leave the small village, the *Albert* had to butt her way through the ice all the way out of the bay. Every time I looked back at the village disappearing in the distance I thought about the misery and pain we were leaving behind. I wondered if anyone would survive during the winter; it was heartbreaking. It haunted me for years."

Dr. Grenfell looked at Judge Squarey as if to ask, "Shall I continue?" The Judge read his expression and nodded.

"Finally we got into open water. As we steamed south at full throttle, Captain Trezise and I started talking about the man we had visited around this time about a year ago, and wondering if he had made it through the winter. Being close to the cove where he lived, we decided to touch in again and pay him a visit.

The only buildings in the cove were owned by a mercantile business out of St. John's, and operated by them during the summer months. There was a wharf, sheds, a retail store and a house where the manager lived during the summer. Further back and almost out of sight was a shack where a winter caretaker lived. When we saw smoke coming from the shack we went in and tied up our vessel. Our intentions were to see who was there and give medical attention if needed.

It is to be pointed out, Your Honour, that this little cove was not a village. It was just a mere rock hole, sheltered by a couple of small islands that absorbed most of the savage swells rolling in from the stormy Labrador Sea. Newfoundland fishermen came here in summer to get supplies.

When the manager closed up the store in the fall he looked for a reliable person or persons to take care of the buildings during the winter. The deal was that the merchant would give them a small portion of rough grub (food) that would help them along during the winter and some firewood. In return, they would take care of the owner's property and do any necessary repairs.

When we arrived at the shack, we found an elderly man who was very pale looking and had a terrible cough. With him was his pet, a black dog called Stony. We asked the man to come south with us to Battle Harbour and get medical treatment, but he refused. We gave him medicine and instructions how to use it. We wished him well and left him.

Now, it was a year later and we were heading south again. On this bitterly cold morning in mid-December, Captain Trezise very cleverly maneuvered the Albert into the cove and we tied up to the wharf. We could see the caretaker's shack in the distance but there was no sign of life. We were about to cast off again when we saw two men walking toward us. Neither of them was the man we'd seen the previous year. Curiously, I stepped up onto the wharf and shook their hands. I told them who I was and what I was doing.

"I suppose you two men are the caretakers," I said as we got ready to leave.

"Yes, we be the caretakers," said one of them. "But we got our crowd with us."

"You two men have your women and children with you?" I said in surprise.

"Yes sir, we do," they said.

I told them I was glad the merchant had the decency to let their families live in his house for the winter.

"Oh no, Doctor, we have our own house built. Look over there," said one of the men. It took a minute or so for Captain Trezise and I to see where their house was, and we only saw it then because we saw smoke coming from the side of the hill.

"We built it by ourselves in less then two days," one man proudly said.

I stared in the direction of what they were calling their home and then turned to Captain Trezise and asked him to spare me a few minutes to go visit the two families. The Captain told me to go ahead. He would wait, although he was pressed for time.

I took my medical bag and went with the two men, walking in ankle deep snow to the sod-covered house protruding from the side of the small hill. As we walked along I asked them if they knew the whereabouts of the man who was there last year.

One of the men spoke up. "Oh, Doctor, you must be talking about Uncle Ike," he said. "He died last winter or early in the spring, starved to death. He ate a dog trying to stay alive or that's what it looked like."

I stopped in my tracks and looked at the men, dumbfounded. "What are you saying?" I asked. They didn't reply and I was going to ask the question again when several dogs started barking loudly and broke the silence. We were now at the entrance to their dwelling. The vicious growling and barking was coming from inside the sod hut they called home.

"Good God in heaven, gentlemen, what do you have in there?" I asked.

"You got no worry about them. Doctor, dar not going to hurt he, dar all penned up," said one of the men.

The older man, who appeared to be in charge, stepped forward and unlatched the porch door and opened it. He walked inside, and in a few seconds he silenced the husky dogs. He invited me inside, but not before warning me that I should keep my head down because of the low ceiling.

I hesitated about going inside, because in the semi-darkness of the porch I could see the snarling huskies through the seams of the boards that made up the pens on either side if the porch. There were eight of these savages stationed there.

I braced myself for what I was going to see inside. I was sure that it would not be very pleasant. Past the stench of urine and the growling of the dogs, I opened another door and stepped into a room that was silent. The men closed the door behind us. It appeared as if there was no one in the room. The only window was one in the roof; streaks of sunlight filtered through the smoke coming from a stovepipe that was partly rusted through. The smell of burning wood was thick in the room.

In this room, there was a low partition dividing the bunk area from the sitting room/kitchen area. The total length and width of the sod hut was about twenty feet by ten feet, including the porch that contained the filthy dog pens.

As my eyes adjusted to the semi-darkness I noticed that everything was spotlessly clean. The floors were made of rough board, but the boards were scrubbed white.

In the tiny kitchen, two women were quietly sitting on wooden benches near the wall. They stood up as I entered. I noticed at first glance that they were both pregnant.

The women wore skin moccasins and long black dresses that hung down to the floor.

"This here is Doctor Grenfell, the one we heard so much about," said the older man as I said good day to the women and shook their hands, trying to make them feel at ease.

I accepted their offer of a cup of tea but said we were pushed for time because of the freeze-up. In a few minutes they had the cup of tea for me. It was raw tea, no milk and no sugar, and I suspected they had none to offer me. I drank it anyway.

One of the women was very talkative. She said they had heard the good news about me being down north. I told them I had been on the coast since June, but had not bothered to come into this cove because I never thought there were women and children living there.

They told me they had only moved here in late October, that they lived further up into the bay. I asked them if I could question them about their pregnancies and have a look at their children. I said I knew they had children because I'd seen the tracks outside in the snow. They told me that they had four children each, ranging in age from one to seven and they were all in good health.

I asked them if the children had any minor sickness such as toothache, earache or dysentery. One of the women spoke up and said, "The youngsters have earache often, but the men take care of that." "What do the men do to cure the earache?" I asked. "Whenever they have 'baccy, they blow 'baccy smoke in their ears, this cures the earache," the woman said. "You mean tobacco?" I said. "Yes," she answered with a laugh. I rolled my eyes in disbelief, but said no more about it.

I asked them where the children were now. The woman doing the talking said they were in the other room. I asked to see them and she went into the other room and brought them out, all eight of them. I was amazed at how well they looked. They were skinny and pale but otherwise strong and healthy. They were very quiet but not shy. They smiled and said hello. After I examined each one, the women sent them back to the other room.

I then proceeded to ask them when they were expecting their babies. One said March, the other February. I asked who would be helping them with the births. They said they would help each other as they had during the births of their other children. I didn't ask any more questions because I was afraid of what I might hear; this was primitive of the highest order."

"It was then that I took out my notebook and wrote in it," said Dr. Grenfell as he reached into his briefcase and took out an old notebook marked 1893-94, Labrador. "This is what I wrote."

This building I am now in is nothing more then a sod hut, a few round sticks and rough board nailed together and covered with sods and mud. It is approx 10 feet by 20 feet with a six-foot high ceiling. It had eight children, two men and two women who are each expecting mothers living here. Also they say that two other adults live here with them but have recently moved up into the bay for a few months trapping. This makes a total of fourteen souls living here. Also, there are eight stinking, half- starved husky dogs penned up in the porch just a few feet away.

"While I was writing, I noticed that the women were staring at my pen and I asked if there was anyone there who could read or write. I was not surprised when they said they had never gone to school. It was sad.

When I was finished writing, I thanked the ladies and went outside, glad for a breath of fresh air. I started walking back to our boat accompanied by the two men. As we walked I asked them more about the man who was there last year, the man they said had starved to death.

"Uncle Ike was our mother's brother, he was very close to us," one answered. "He died in late April or early May, he starved to death after finishing all the food the merchant had left for him. On the last of it he even ate his pet dog, old Stony, trying to stay alive."

After walking a few more steps, he stopped and said, "Just a minute Doctor Grenfell." I stopped and saw that they were looking at a little clearing not far away. "Come here, Doctor, we will show you his grave," said the older man as we walked over to the clearing and they took off their caps. "This is his grave, my brother and I put up this cross for Uncle Ike and Stony, his old dog." The cross was clearly visible on the snow-covered grave; I bent down and read the words scribbled on it:

"TO UNCLE IKE AND OLD STONY"

I added as a prayer, "May God rest their souls."

One of the men turned to me and said there was more to the story than what they had told me and I said I'd like to hear the rest.

"In the spring," he said, "when the fish merchant came back again he went into the shack where Uncle Ike used to live in the winter time. When he opened the door he smelled a terrible stink and saw something over on the wooden bunk wrapped in an old dirty blanket. He pulled it back and there were the remains of Uncle Ike. The merchant sent word for us up in the bay to come out and bury him because we were his relatives. We came out and sure enough Uncle Ike was dead. When we went in the cabin we found something else. In a wooden box near his bunk we found the bones of Stony, his dog. The bones were as clean as a whistle, even the skull was scooped out and boiled clean, there wasn't even any skin left around the teeth, everything was picked clean and eaten. We took all Stony's bones and put them inside Uncle Ike's coat, then wrapped their remains in old brim bags that the fish merchant gave us and brought them here and buried them," the man finished by looking up at the sky and saying, "May God rest their souls."

At that moment I was very shaken. I figured I had heard it all. I said a prayer for the man and his dog. Then they told me there was lots of food locked away in the merchant's store just a few feet from where Ike had starved. I stared at them in disbelief. We walked down to the wharf in silence. When we got to the schooner I told them to wait on the wharf until I got some things for them. I gave them medicine, and things for the women's needs, also earache drops and toothache drops for the children. Captain Trezise came up with a wooden box full of things for the children, some candy and a few toys. In a few weeks it would be Christmas. Before we cast off our lines, I shook hands with the men. I remember the last words I said to them was, "Men, for God's sake, please look after your women and children."

As we cast off, I looked in the direction of the sod hut and saw the two women and the eight children standing outside waving at us and calling goodbye. I waved back to them. Tears filled my eyes as I said to Captain Trezise, "I can't see how they will ever be able to survive in that hut to see spring." In a few moments we were gone. This was the last time I ever saw any of them."

Grenfell wiped tears from his eyes. "Your Honour," he said, "the story doesn't end here."

"You may continue, Dr. Grenfell," said Judge Squarey. And he and everyone else waited silently and tearfully for Grenfell to regain his composure and continue.

"The following summer I was again on the Labrador Coast and steaming along by the same little outpost. I'd thought about the two families we had left there more then a thousand times during the winter back home in England and wondered if they had survived. I asked the Captain to touch in, I wanted to check and see. After we tied up the vessel I went ashore and walked up a grassy lane. It looked much different now then it had in December. Everything was green with short grass and shrubs. I saw the sod hut on the hillside. I went up to the door but all was silent, it was obvious to me that no one was inside but the stench of the huskies was still evident.

I turned and started to head back to our vessel, but thought about the grave of Uncle Ike and Stony and decided to pay them one last visit. As I walked to the little grassy knoll where the wooden cross stood in the sunshine, I noticed another newly erected cross standing nearby. I knelt down in front of it and read the scribbled words written in blue lumber crayon:

IN LOVING MEMORY OF MAGGIE AGE 36 YEARS
AND HER BELOVED DAUGHTER
THEY BOTH DIED FEBUARY 20
GONE TO THEIR REST

Maggie was the older of the two women and she had died giving birth to her child. My heart was broken and I wept openly. As I turned and walked toward my vessel, I saw the merchant standing silently on the shop step. He wore a quiff hat, and smiled at me as I passed. He must have seen my tears because he never said hello. I stepped aboard our vessel and headed out wondering what in God's name I would see next."

CHAPTER 30
Domino

K nowing Dr. Grenfell would not be able to immediately continue his testimony, Judge Squarey called a two-hour recess before proceeding with questioning him:

Q. Have these co-op stores ever interfered with trade to any great extent?"

A. Only in legitimate competition. They get nearly everything they sell in St. John's. I don't think that any of these people import anything direct.

Q. To your knowledge, have any clothes given by Americans or any outsiders been passed over to these stores?"

A. Never. No garment has ever been passed over.

The Judge questioned Dr. Grenfell about the workings of the machine shop, book-keeping, and method of payment by patients both rich and poor. He then questioned him about the religious aspect of the work.

Q. What missionary work do you do?

A. Well, everything we do is missionary work. We have never employed a clergyman of any denomination. I do not believe in employing them.

Q. Do you preach yourself?

A. If I am asked to do so.

Q. Do you give lectures?

A. Yes. I have no church. I give Sunday afternoon services.

Q. Are you asked by the Church of England and the Methodists to help them conduct their services?

A. At times. The work embraces all denominations and no denominations. We look at a man's qualifications when we select a doctor. We do not select a surgeon because he can preach.

Q. Tell this Commission, Dr. Grenfell, if you can recall, where your Medical Mission first began here in this Colony and what convinced you to stay?

A. There was a certain incident just after I arrived on the Labrador Coast that convinced me to stay. I always say that Domino was where I really started my Medical Mission in Newfoundland and Labrador.

I had gone into a place called Snug Harbour around the second week in June, just after I came here, and learned there was a very sick child there. I found the young child was on the verge of dying with appendicitis and had no choice but to operate in order to save her life.

While performing the operation in her house, I was told about a man not far away who had shot his wife and children that past winter to prevent them from starving. I'm not going to repeat the story because it is too graphic. I told it one time on BBC Radio in London and was accused of lying to the public.

We stayed in Snug Harbour for two days caring for the young child. Two days later, after battling heavy ice, we arrived at Domino.

The harbour was full of schooners waiting for the ice to break up so that they could go further north to their summer fishing places.

People flocked to us all day with their illnesses. Late in the evening, when the rush of visitors to our vessel was over, I came up on deck to look around. I was lost in thought as I looked at the rugged schooners that surrounded us.

I suddenly noticed a small rowboat pushing toward us. On closer inspection, I saw it was a bunch of slabs nailed together with tar smeared on the seams to help make it float. I waved to the person in the contraption to come closer, I was curious to get a better look at the craft. It moved toward me until it got within fifty feet then stopped. I looked at the poor wretched soul sitting quietly in the craft and saw it was just a young boy. He had brown hair and a tanned face and he sat up straight holding two oars. I estimated he was no more than thirteen or fourteen years old. He wore raggedy clothes that looked to be much too large for him.

I motioned for him to come a little closer and he did. Then looked up at me and said in a weak voice, "Do you be a real doctor, sir?

"That is what they call me," I said.

"Us hasn't got any m-m-money at all, sir," he stammered. "But there's a dying man ashore and mom sent me to see if you would come and have a look at 'un if you could."

The boy looked to be malnourished, skittish and filthy. His hair was long and his hands were covered in dirt. He looked at me with desperation on his face. "Yes, I certainly will come and look at him," I said.

We launched a small boat, and I called my assistant, Harry Taylor, to come with me. "Take us to the sick man," I said to the young boy.

When we got on shore we climbed up to a sod-covered shack perched on the side of a cliff. I could hardly believe that people lived there. We followed the boy in through a heavy plank door and saw inside a floor made of beach sand and mud spread between flat rocks to make it an even surface. There were pieces of broken glass stuck up in front of holes that they used for windows. It was like walking into a dungeon. The young boy closed the door behind us.

When we entered the house and stood in the semi- darkness I noticed a rusty old stove standing in the corner with an iron stovepipe going up through a hole in the roof. Along the wall on one side were two tiers of bunks with children in them looking frightened and neglected. They stared at us with wide eyes. In a bunk on the other side of the house was a man lying in a crude bed who was coughing his heart out and appeared to be very sick and weak. Sitting on a wooden bench near him was a frail looking woman dressed in rags, feeding him some broth with a spoon. There was no sound except for the man's coughing. I introduced Harry Taylor and myself to the woman and told her I was a doctor.

She held out her hand and said hello, then moved away from her sick husband.

I opened my medical bag and took out my stethoscope and proceeded to examine the patient. He had a high fever and his heart rate and pulse were completely out of control. I knew he had pneumonia from the sound of his lungs. It was also apparent that he had tuberculosis. There was a bucket near the bed that he had been using to spit into. The woman had this covered with a heavy piece of rag. I surveyed the room and as my heart sank to the lowest ebb of my life I knew this was no place for a sick man. I thought about taking him aboard the *Albert* and admitting him to the little hospital ward we had there. But I knew it was too late, the man was dying.

I prayed with him and asked him if he had made his peace with God. He replied in a weak voice that it was the only thing he ever had to look forward to in his whole life. I gave him a shot of morphine for pain. As I stood there looking at the conditions he and his family lived in my heart ached. I thought again about telling the family I would take their husband and father on board our boat but decided not to. If he died a day or so after leaving Domino, with a solid jam of ice blocking our return, we might have to bury him in an unmarked grave somewhere along the coast or even at sea. For that reason, I decided it would be better to leave him and let him die with his family. It would be unthinkable to sail away with this man and not bring him back again.

I asked the woman who was going to provide for her and her family while her husband was sick, she said she didn't know. She said they were out of food and only living on what people around were giving them. She said the schooners traveling to and from the northern coast gave them salt fish and a little food, enough to keep them alive. My soul cried out in vain but there was nothing I could do, only walk away. There was no place where they could get Government assistance or any kind of social help. I told her that I would try and get word to the authorities to give her assistance; this was like foreign language to her.

I gathered the family around me and prayed, there was nothing else I could do. I left and went back to our vessel with the young boy in tow. We took him aboard and gave him a complete change of clothes. We also gave him medicine for his father and enough food to last the family for about a month.

In my notes, I recorded that a couple of months later I returned to Domino on my way South. I went ashore because I was anxious to know what had happened to the sick man. As I neared the shack, I saw the woman standing in the doorway. She appeared to be in a worse state then when we were here before. She told me her husband had passed away the day after we left. This poor widow, who had nothing, was now responsible for caring for a family of six. I wrote the Government after we left and about a month later she had a dole order from St. John's that she took to the floating merchant who gave her a little food.

I asked the woman what her plans were for the coming winter. She said she didn't know, that she would have to stay there because she had no other place to go. I offered to take her and her children anywhere she wanted to go but she repeated she had no other place to go. Before we left I gave her almost all the food we had aboard the *Albert*. I gave them medicine too and said goodbye.

As we left Domino, I asked God to open up a way so that I would never again have to turn my back on a desolate family anywhere on the Labrador. I asked for guidance to start an orphanage and a hospital and my prayer has been answered ten-fold. I never saw nor heard of that family again although I inquired about them many times afterwards.

When Dr. Grenfell finished telling the story there wasn't a dry eye in the room. After a moment's silence, Grenfell rose and asked Judge Squarey if the story he'd told about Domino not be recorded as part of his evidence. He feared someone might think he was looking for sympathy in order to sway the Commission. The Judge said he would strike the story about Domino from the record, as well as the one about Rigolet.

CHAPTER 31

Grenfell

The rest of the testimony given by Dr. Grenfell centered on the operations of the hospitals and the Medical Mission. Just before Judge Squarey closed the hearings at St. Anthony he asked Dr. Grenfell if there was anything else he wanted to say. Grenfell said there was and was told to go ahead:

"Your Honour," Grenfell said in his lecturing tone of voice as he stood up to address Judge Squarey. "After I first came here in the summer of 1892, I saw the medical situation around the Northern part of Newfoundland and along the coast of Labrador. While reviewing the medical situation I found that a greater problem existed then the one surrounding the medical crisis. As I moved around from village to village, from outport to outport, in every bay and cove I found destitute people, sickness, starvation, oppression, illiteracy, abuse in every sense of the word. I found a population desperate and starving and unable to do anything about it. We did a survey and found that more than 20,000 people left Newfoundland and went to Labrador for the summer fishery. We found too that the permanent residents were abused and mistreated by the fish merchants. One of the worst things we found was that Labrador had no representation in the House of Assembly. One either had to have enough influence to be able to talk to the Governor or the Prime Minister in order to raise a complaint. Ninety-nine per cent of the population could not read or write. When we first went to Labrador we found horrible living conditions and no medical facilities.

We looked around and saw the floating merchants in their big vessels and were amazed to find they had no one with medical knowledge on board. It could have been so easy for the merchants and the Government to have a vessel manned by medical staff and sent to Labrador in the spring. At least, people would have someone to turn to during the summer. I suggested this to the Prime Minister in the fall of 1892 but he just shrugged it off. With this response, we decided to do it ourselves. We started hospitals, nursing stations, orphanages, schools, farms, industrial shops, and of course we showed the people how to start cooperatives, cash stop stores and trained them how to run them. We also started a host of other things, including sending people to different parts of the world to train in different fields. Most of them have returned and are working, either with us or in their own businesses. Above it all, it has been a trying time, but very rewarding. This is my final remark. We thank you for listening to our statements and concerns and hope it will all be said and done for the benefit of mankind. Thank you."

"We thank you also, Dr. Grenfell, for your cooperation and enlightenment. We're sure that the final results of this Commission will greatly benefit the Colony of Newfoundland and Labrador. Thank you. This court will now be adjourned," said Squarey.

CHAPTER 32

To Battle Harbour

E arly the next morning the Commission of Enquiry left St. Anthony and headed for Battle Harbour, Labrador, where the first sparks for the enquiry had been ignited. Immediately upon arrival, Judge Squarey summoned Dr. Charles Curtis.

Examined by Mr. Hunt, the witness said as follows:

I am a Doctor of Medicine, A.B. Clark University and M.D. of Harvard. I have been practicing for four years. For sixteen months I was House Surgeon to Boston City Hospital, six months Surgeon to Boston Lying-in Hospital, six months instructor of obstetrics at Yale Medical School, and with the Grenfell Mission two years. I was a year at St. Anthony. Last summer I was on the Strathcona. Since June I have been here at Battle Harbour. I am in charge here. I have had as assistants, one third-year medical student of Harvard University, three graduate nurses and one graduated dentist. Since June we have had at the hospital ninety in-patients and six hundred and fifty out-patients. We have preformed about forty operations under ether; eight of them were major operations, such as abdominal surgery. I have made a special study of the diseases of women and during the summer I have done several operations of that character.

We get our supplies for the hospital from St. John's. There have been no supplies imported by us this summer.

There is a cooperative store here; I have bought supplies from it this summer to the value of $60. I have no personal knowledge of how it works. Services are conducted on Sunday by me or by one of the medical students. The services are open to the public. They are just ordinary services, no special forms.

We also purchase goods from the other business here at Battle Harbour as well as from the cooperative store. That is the ordinary course of business.

To my knowledge there has never been any clothing sold for cash. I am the one in charge of it all. We give away most of it, for instance, a widow of eighty just came here from Fox Harbour, and she was very destitute. We gave her clothes and bedding before she left. There has never been any clothing that was given to the Mission transferred to the cooperative stores for sale, or anything else since I have been here in charge, nor will there be any. All clothing that comes here has been cleared through customs at St. John's.

It has been compulsory for our casual employees to take clothing this summer because there has been no money to pay them for their work. It is understood by them in advance that they will be paid in clothing. Those who sell us fish or fire- wood understand the same. We pay 10 cents a pound for salmon and 10 cents for each cod fish, dried of course.

The hospital was not kept open last winter and it won't be open this winter. Last winter there was no doctor here, it will be the same this winter. It is impossible to heat the wards with firewood during the winter due to no trees on the island.

We plan to build a new hospital about ten miles from here further up into Lewis Bay near the heavy forest where it is sheltered.

Sworn at Battle Harbour
Charles L. Curtis, M.D.

The next witness was a William Belbin who stated under oath:

I belong to Bay Roberts, Newfoundland, where I live. I am lighthouse keeper at Double Island lighthouse, Battle Harbour. The lighthouse is operated from June first to the last of November. My son and daughter live with me at the lighthouse. My son is my assistant. I have been working this lighthouse for nine years. None of my family has been treated at the hospital during the time I have been here, or by any of the doctors connected with the hospital. My son was sick last summer with the measles. He was unconscious for three days. I wrote Dr. Grieve, who was at that time medical superintendent. I have no copy of my letter to Dr. Grieve. I said in my letter that my boy was taken bad with the measles and asked if he would come and see him. I produce Dr. Grieve's reply (see below). The boy recovered, he was ill for three weeks. That was the only time that I asked for medical assistance except once when my daughter was a little sick and she went in the hospital. She came out the same day. The doctor examined her and sent her right back again. She was treated kindly at the hospital. I do not know how many patients were at the hospital when my son was ill with the measles.

Sworn and signed. William Belbin.

Letter written to William Belbin:

The International Grenfell Association
INCORPORATED

July 3/16.
Dear Mr. Belbin:
I understand your son has measles, this being the case; I cannot attend him on account of possibly infecting patients in the hospital.
The treatment of measles themselves is very simple; you must keep the boy warm and keep him indoors for a week after the measles have disappeared.

Yours faithfully,
John Grieve.

Judge Squarey next interviewed Michael Grady who said under oath:

I belong to and live in Carbonear. I am a fisherman. I fish in Mattie's Cove, in Battle Harbour. I have a wife and two children. Last summer I applied for medical assistance to Dr. Grieve for one of my children. My little girl had measles. I asked the doctor to come over and see the little girl. He said he would not like to come over because it may flood the hospital with measles. I made the application in person. There were a few blotches on the child's face. She was weak on her legs. She was three years old. The next day, or the next day after I brought the child to the hospital. The Doctor told me to take her out of the hospital and take her home, to wrap her up in warm blankets and that should be all right. I took her home. She died two days later. Dr. Grieve told me then that she died of pneumonia. He had not seen the child who died. Two days later my other child took it. I sent to Dr. Grieve again. He made no objection to coming to see the other one. He treated the other child and cured her. He gave the other child something to keep down the fever.

Under further examination by Mr. Hunt, Grady said:

It was on the wharf that the Doctor first told me that the first child died of pneumonia. Dr. Grieve did his best for the other child. The child got a cold moving her out of the house to the hospital. After the child was brought back from the hospital she took to screeching and died that way. When I came to the hospital first, he gave me medicine to take for diarrhea. When he would not come to the house to look at the child I brought her to the hospital. I brought her of my own free will. The Doctor did not ask me to bring the child to the hospital. When I left the hospital the first day, he told me to keep the child warm and that she would be all right. Dr. Grieve attended my brother and cured him. He had erysipelas of the face. He was very attentive to him.

Examined by Mr. Emerson, Grady said:

When I saw the Doctor the first time he told me to wrap the child up warm. The wind was in from the northeast and it was a cold day when I brought the child over to the hospital. The child was wrapped up in warm blankets as warm as we could get it. The second child that he cured was five years old.

The next witness was Isaac Cumby. Upon examination by Mr. Emerson he said:

I belong to Indian Cove. I am a fisherman. About three or four years ago I obtained some Springfield rifles from Dr. Grenfell. They were given to me to sell. I gave the money to Dr. Grieve. I do not know what they cost originally. I sold them for six dollars each. There were thirty Springfield rifles, which I sold at six dollars each, and one other kind, which I sold for ten dollars. I do not know the caliber of this rifle it was not very big. I sold them to the fishermen. They were used for killing seals and deer. I do not know if the duty was paid on them or not. I never heard any questions of duty raised afterwards.

Upon examination by Mr. Hunt, Cumby said:

If there was anything done in connection with the duties I had nothing to do with it. If the matter received the attention of the customs I do not know anything about it. I just took the rifles and had no discussion about the payment of the duties. When the proceeds were handed over to Dr. Grieve, that finished my connection with them. I just sold them for Dr. Grenfell.

Upon examination by the Commissioner, Cumby said:

Dr. Grenfell gave me the rifles to sell for him. He fixed the price at $7 each.

The testimony of Alexander Dwyer, under oath
Examined by Mr. Emerson

I am a sergeant of police, and for some years have been doing duty on the Labrador, that is the south coast. I have a general knowledge of the Grenfell Association. I was stationed at St. Anthony in the summer of 1910 for six months. The following year I was there for a fortnight or three weeks. I have been doing duty with the Magistrate on the Labrador Coast for seven summers. In the course of that duty and as inspector of weights and measures I have called upon the ports at which the Grenfell Association operates. I have never detected any breaches of the law on the part of the Association; I knew that fishermen and other laborers at the hospital and mission buildings were paid in clothing for their work. I brought this to the attention of Mr. Kelly Morrissey one year and he said that the government was well aware of it.

On one occasion I received clothing from the Mission Store. I bought some vegetables once at the request of Mr. Ruben Simms and which I forwarded to the Mission. Subsequently I received clothing for my children for these vegetables. I brought them on to St. John's. The constable that I was with, brought the matter to the notice of the Inspector General. He took my bag and I never seen it since. That is the only time that I ever received anything from the Mission. I have never known the Mission to sell goods for cash. At one time when I went there first and before I knew the difference, a man named Penney offered me an order which he had on the store for goods, but before I presented it found out that it was against the rules of the Association to transfer these orders. So I had nothing to do with it. I only know of one instant in which a man sold an order and I understand he lost his job in the mission when they discovered it. There was a notice posted in the office at that time, at least I think there was, in any case it was an understood thing, that anyone who transferred his order would lose his job.

It was two years ago that I received this clothing from the Mission. Mr. Kelly Morrissey was the inspector of customs at that time. When I heard from him that the Government was well aware that the Mission gave clothes for labour and provisions I knew it would be wrong on my part to accept clothing from them for vegetables even thought I had a large family of eight children. Mr. Morrissey had seen dozens of people having goods given to them on orders for work and wages. It was my intention to obtain clothing for my children in exchange for the vegetables. It would not have paid for me to take cash for them. I know of no case in which goods sent to the Mission was transferred to the cooperative stores. I remember one occasion where three cases of guns were landed from a Halifax vessel, addressed to the cooperative store. I do not know if duty was paid or not, but I remember asking Dr. Grenfell for one of the guns to locate a man who was suspected of trapping out of season. The Doctor told me I could not get the gun until they were inspected by Mr. Simms, the Customs officer. After Simms had inspected the rifles, I got one.

Examined by Mr. Emerson, Dwyer said:

When I said that it would not pay me to take cash for the vegetables that I sent to the Mission, I meant that I knew what kind of clothing they had in the store and the prices in the shop. The facts of the whole transaction are these. When I say that the vegetables were for the Mission, I mean that Mr. Simms, the storekeeper of the Mission, asked me to get them. Mr. Simms had a large family and his children worked at the Mission, as did he also. Some of the vegetables, which he wanted, were for him and some of the Mission institutions. I was to be paid for what I sent to the Mission from the Mission store in clothing. The vegetables that I sent to Mr. Simms personally were to be paid for by him out of the clothing which he had received from the store for his children, and which did not suit him.

I am almost positive that the rifles referred to were sent addressed to the cooperative store, where some of them were sold. I don't know what happened to the remainder. I think a man named Webster of New York, who was connected with the Mission, off and on, was manager of the cooperative store that year. I asked Dr. Grenfell for the loan of one of the guns, because he and the JP were sending me in the bay to investigate the trapper who was breaking the law.

CHAPTER 33

John Croucher

The examination of John Croucher was taken under oath at Battle Harbour, Sept. 27, 1917. Examined by Mr. Emerson, Croucher said he had been manager for Baine Johnston at Battle Harbour and vicinity for twenty years. He continued:

When I came here the Grenfell Mission was established in a very small way. At that time they had a small house in the eastern end of the present hospital belonging to Baine Johnston Company which they were using for a small hospital and a dwelling house for the Doctor. In 1901, they built the southern annex and later added to the old building by raising the roof. In 1905 they built the Doctor's house and in 1906 they built the laundry. The land upon which the hospital is built and also the other buildings belongs to Baine Johnston & Co. Originally Mr. W.B. Grieve gave them the use of the house upon which they started provided it was not used for anything else except a hospital. There were no documents that I know of. The Mission obtained permission to build upon the land where the hospital now is and where the Doctor's house and laundry now are from Mr. Grieve. Permission was obtained upon the same conditions as I have stated. I believe that the Mission has recently obtained from Mr. Grieve a written lease of these lands. The work of the Mission since I have been here has consisted in the giving of medical and surgical aid, the holding of religious services on Sundays, the distribution of clothing amongst people. The medical and surgical work of the Mission as a whole has been admired and I have nothing to say against it. I know of the case of a man named Chubbs who came here suffering from tuberculosis. When he arrived there were no nurses and he was refused admission to the hospital. He died in the boat at the wharf here. I would not say it was neglect, but it was not very charitable, to say the least. That was two or three years ago. Dr. Grieve was in charge of the Hospital at the time.

I know of no objection to their holding religious services. They are not in any way offensive to the people.

The distribution of clothing was in operation when I came here, on a smaller scale than it is now. I have no figures, but I should say that the increase has been large. The American end of the Mission was not then in operation and everything then was done in England. In any case the Mission was very much smaller. The goods which they distributed were clothing. When the goods came from England we brought most of it out and saw it; now it comes by rail and steamer and we do not see it. When I came here we used to keep stock of ready-made clothing of which we used to sell quite a bit. Now we hardly keep any ready-mades. We sell perhaps ten or twelve suits in a year. I do not think that the sale of underclothing has been affected very much. Until the cooperative store started here we had no competitor in trade. The cooperative store opened in 1915. The sale of ready-mades had fallen before that. The loss of this business was not caused by trade competition. The material prosperity is undoubtedly better than it was twenty years ago. The earnings of the people have practically doubled. There ought to be a greater sale for everything than there was then. There is no other factor that would interfere with our business except the distribution of clothing. I never complained of any illegality in that. As far as I know it is all traded, anybody who brings anything for it can obtain it. I have seen it on a good many and the great proportion of them could afford to pay for their clothing. I have not got the remotest idea of the value of the clothing distributed.

Up to the last seven or eight years the relations of my firm with the Mission have been perfectly friendly. My firm has always acted generously towards the Mission. They have carried out goods for them free of charges. We never charged them a cent. We have allowed them to use our premises for landing goods and any steamer belonging to the Mission coming here always come into our wharf. They use our cranes and if they wanted any men we always gave them assistance. My personal relations with the Mission and the members of the staff up to that time were always friendly. The first cause of friction was when the present Doctor here, Dr. Grieve, induced some of our dealers to send to St. John's direct for their goods. In some cases to entrust him with their money to buy the goods for them. I do not question the legality of the proceeding but in view of the way in which the firm had always acted towards him personally and towards the Mission it was hardly the proper thing to do. It lasted until Dr. Grieve went away to Harrington. His successor did not pursue the same practice. On Dr. Grieve's return, he was chiefly instrumental in starting the cooperative stores in competition with us and again I do not question the legality of that but only its propriety. So far the cooperative store has not injured my trade very much, nor has it caused us any inconvenience. I do not know anything about the class of goods they carry. From what the fishermen tell us, their prices are about alike. Several shareholders of the cooperative store deal with us still.

I am also postmaster here. A good many parcels come for members of the Mission staff and are all admitted duty free. The decision as to whether they are to come in duty free is made before the parcels arrive here.

I saw a copy of the petition presented by the International Grenfell Association to the House of Assembly last session. In reference to paragraph 8 of that petition and speaking as one with considerable experience in the Labrador trade, I would say that there is no truth whatsoever in the statement that mercantile firms and persons trading on the Labrador has ever exploited the people of this region. In fact the boot is on the other foot. To a great extent the business done by mercantile firms is done on credit. To supply the fishermen with enough provisions clothing and implements to carry on their trade and with salt in the hope they will be paid in fish when it is caught. The payment for the goods so given is dependent upon the success of the fishery. We take the fish at a price fixed in accordance with the conditions of the foreign markets to which the fish is exported. That market fluctuates considerably. So that there is the additional risk that after obtaining the fish at the price fixed that loss may occur in the sale of the fish. We also take whatever other fish is caught by our dealers at the same price and take our chance on the fluctuations of foreign markets in the sale of that. There is therefore considerable risk in the business and the fishermen are dependent upon our trading in this way for their existence.

The Mission and its officers have been aware that our business has been carried on with absolute fairness towards our dealers. They know that our accounts have been furnished to them and that they have always received cash for their balance. Our firm and all its officers have always assisted in every way to forward the surgical and medical end of the work and whilst we have never questioned the legality of the Mission's work or the actions of their employees, we certainly question the friendliness of their acts in stimulating these cooperative stores and being the instigation of them.

As postmaster it has come under my notice that medical students of whom there are six or eight every year down here, import free of duty expensive sweets and luxuries. I do not think that this ought to be so as I do not consider them officers of the Mission.

Examined by Mr. Hunt, Croucher said:

I have no complaint whatever to make against the religious or medical work of the Mission. In connection with the Chubbs matter I was not here at the time and what I have stated I have merely heard. It is possible that the hospital people had some reason for not admitting Chubbs. There were no nurses here at the time. Chubbs lived at Seal Bight. I do not know that Dr. Grieve made a special komatik trip to see him in the winter. On the whole their record is a good one. They are the only medical assistance down here. Mr. Grieve of our firm was a subscriber to the Mission fund. I understand he contributed liberally, both in money and services. Dr Grieve bound up my legs one time when I went overboard. The Doctors have always treated my family and men very well. When I stated that the great proportion of the clothes given out by the Mission was given out to those that could afford to pay for them. I do not wish it to be understood that I consider this illegal or that I have any objections to it for I have none whatsoever. With reference to the orders for goods that went to St. John's, I cannot say what they amounted to. It is only natural that a person in business would want to sell all the goods that he can. As far as I know, the Mission has never done anything illegal. I am the only other store here besides the cooperative store. I presume that at the present time the cooperative store does the larger part of the business that was formerly done through St. John's. My business has not dropped that I know of.

Speaking as post-master, I may say that duty on parcels is assessed before it comes to Battle Harbour and it is not for me to decide whether duty is to be paid or not. I cannot say that goods coming to the cooperative stores have not paid duty.

I remember the firm bringing over fifteen tons of salt from Ireland for Dr. Grenfell. This was Irish salt and was used for experimental purposes. It was given to the planters but it proved a failure for the curing of the fish as it left yellow sediment upon them. There was none of it sold.

I do not know if the cooperative stores have ever sold goods sent to the Mission for charitable purposes.

Sworn before me at Battle Harbour this 27th day of September 1917.

CHAPTER 34

William Soper

W illiam Soper, who had a business at Cape Charles, was one of the very few who had negative things to say about the Grenfell Mission. He stated he had signed the petition and wanted an enquiry for one reason: to look into what he called "the co-op racket."

In his testimony, he said he had been on the Labrador for sixty years and had seen it all. But, he said, the worst that ever happened to him was when the co-op started next door to him. "By the establishment of the cooperative store here at Cape Charles, my business has been ruined."

He went on to say, "I am speaking with sixty years experience of being on the Labrador, I can say positively that the people of Labrador have not been exploited by mercantile firms...I understood that the Grenfell Mission was established here to bring medical aid to the people and to assist the poor. For some years they confined themselves to that work. But now they are gone into the fish business, and have been at it for three years...There has been no improvement in the welfare of the people by establishing these co-ops...I've got no complaints with the medical work here. I would say that they have done a good job. My only complaint is about the distribution of clothing and the establishing of the co-op stores... I am the only business here outside of the co-op, if they were not here the people would have to buy from me, and I would take their fish."

CHAPTER 35

St. John's

The Commission conducted many other interviews in different locations around Labrador. Most people said the same thing, that the Grenfell Mission and the cooperative stores were a blessing to the whole coast, in every aspect. No one wanted to see anything moved or tampered with. The Commissioner and his entourage then left Labrador and returned to St. John's to continue the hearings which started on October 17, 1917.

The first person to be summoned was Father George Thibault Parish Priest of Conche, Newfoundland who stated:

I have been parish priest for the Mission of Conche for ten years. I am acquainted with the workings of the Grenfell Mission. I have visited the hospital at St. Anthony. I was the guest of Dr. Fallon, medical Supertendent of the Mission, and lodged at the hospital. Dr. Fallon showed me around the premises and in my capacity as priest I tended some of the patients there. As far as I have seen, there is no discrimination whatsoever between any denominations. All receive equal treatment. None of my people have ever complained of any treatment they received at the Mission. I would have heard of any complaint if any had been made. When I first went down there it was Dr. Grenfell who took me around my mission in his own steamer. Since then we have been on the best of terms. Although I have had intimate knowledge of the workings of the Mission, I have never seen or known of any possible cause for complaint. I regard the Mission as a blessing to the coast. It has my warmest wishes for its success. It would be a bad day for Labrador and Northern Newfoundland if it ceased its operations. I have seen a great change for the better in the condition of the people in the last ten years, which in a great measure can be attributed to the Mission.

The next witness was Reverend Henry Gordon who stated:

I am a Church of England Missionary at Cartwright, Labrador. I am attached to the Diocese of Newfoundland. I have been in the Diocese for over two years and have been in Labrador about two years. I am a native of England and M.A. of Oxford. I have been in touch to a certain extent with the Grenfell Mission Association. As for medical work, it appears to be very good. Its influence on the people from a social point of view is also good, mainly through the personal influence and example of the mission workers and the advice and assistance given to the people. I think the general condition of the people has improved by it. I have come principally in touch with Dr. Paddon and the work of the station at Indian Harbour and also at North West River in the winter. I have high personal regard for him and a good opinion of his work. The operation of the Association gives the people a good deal of employment, of which there was very little before. As far as I have seen, the work of the mission has not interfered with the religious ideas of my people in any way. They have not lost any of their interest in their own church since the association has been inaugurated. I have heard of no complaints of any such things among the people themselves. On one occasion they transported me from North West River to Rigolet, a distance of ninety miles. In my experience no member of the mission has ever made any attempt to proselytize.

The staff is composed of persons of very high character. As far as I can understand a good many of them are volunteers, working without remuneration.

Next was Edwin Grant, who had been carrying on a business at Blanc Sablon, Quebec for the past 33 years. In testimony given October 17, 1917, he said:

When I went there first the Grenfell Mission had not been established. The nearest cooperative store to Blanc Sablon is Red Bay, 36 miles away. That store has not interfered with my business at all. The nearest hospital is at Forteau, about nine miles away. At that hospital they also distribute clothing. That distributing of clothing does not interfere with my sales at all. The distribution is not to those people who would naturally buy from me.

Examined by Mr. Dunfield, Grant said:

I should say that the Mission is a great benefit to the people on the whole. I have had occasion to call upon the nurse at Forteau several times and have sent several patients to the hospital at Bateau this year. Cooperative stores do not affect my stores in any way. In fact, I was the one that asked Dr. Grenfell to establish a cooperative store at Forteau where I trade. I consider that the advantage to the people would completely outweigh the disadvantage to me, personally, of competition in trade. I consider that the general improvement in the condition would in any case be good for trade in the long run. I think that the cooperative store at Flowers Cove has done well for the people there. I think that competition everywhere has done well.

On October 27, Mr. Emerson called upon Josiah Gosse who stated:

I am a Customs officer on board a vessel touring the Labrador Coast. I have held that position for eight years. I have been in touch with the north coast of Labrador and the Northern Peninsula all my life. I remember when the Grenfell Mission came to Newfoundland. I have knowledge of the hospital work they have been doing along the coast. The work that they do in that direction is very good. They do very good service.

I am also a relieving officer on the coast. My jurisdiction extends from Battle Harbour north to wherever we go. In regard to the charge made by the petitioners to the House of Assembly that the Grenfell Mission has been trading on the Labrador, my view of the customs act is that goods imported for chartable purposes free of duty should be given away in charity. If any return is taken for them it is a sale. I understand that the Grenfell Association gets a return for these goods.

In reference to the incident where guns were imported by Dr. Grenfell for the Association some five or six years ago, I received an intimation that these guns were imported by the Grenfell Association. In answer to my enquiry the authorities in town informed me that no duty had been paid on them. Dr. Grieve sold these guns. I summoned Isaac Cumby for buying one of the guns and Dr. Grieve for a breach of the Custom Act. The case was partly heard, and for some reason or the other the case was postponed. When I came back to St. John's I reported it to the Customs. That is the last I heard of it. In the fall of 1912, goods were taken onboard the "Invermore" at Battle Harbour belonging to the Mission and taken down to Mr. Swaffield, the Hudson Bay store's agent. Mr. Swaffield's instructions from Dr. Grenfell were that none of his goods were to be given out without return. In the early summer of 1913, Miss Luther of the Grenfell Mission brought onboard at Rigolet a bag full of skin cuffs, the work of the natives of Labrador, being the return for these goods. I saw her selling to the American tourists on that trip, skin cuffs for $1.50, which could be purchased from the natives for 40 cents. I asked Dr. Wakefield what happened to this money. He said it went to the upkeep of the Mission. These are the only incidents which I can recollect, either of trading or of breaches of the Custom Act. As Relieving Officer I sometimes come in contact with officials of the Mission. They sometimes recommend to me cases worthy of consideration. I never recommend any cases to them. I have asked women and children who have come aboard poorly clad whether they have received any goods from the mission, and they have said no. The duties of a relieving officer are a very difficult one; it is hard to please everyone. But during my eight years on the coast I have managed to give satisfaction to the natives and to the Newfoundland fishermen who go down there and to the Government, but I have never been able to give satisfaction to the officials of the Mission. They have been making complaints all the time, but now I have got so used to it that I don't mind it at all.

Examined by Mr. Dunfield, the witness said as follows:

It was August 31, 1912 that I issued a summons against Dr. Grieve worded as follows. "For that you did in the winter of 1912 commit a breach of the Custom Act Sec. 96. The summons does not state any place at which the offense was committed. The offense in relation to which this summons was issued was selling guns, one to a man named Cumby. I do not remember if he had any other cases down here at that time, on which I thought duty had not been paid. Magistrate Joseph H. Penney issued the summons. It was dated August 30th at twelve o'clock. The policeman Mr. Dwyer served it. That was on a Friday, the summons was for Saturday. I do not remember what time of the day the summons was issued. One Frank Lewis now dead, winter agent for Baine Johnston, told me that guns had been brought over from St. Anthony the previous fall for Dr. Grieve to sell. I filled in the summons sitting at Magistrate Penney's desk on board the boat. I do not remember whether I filled it in before he signed it or after. That was the information on which I got out the summons. I did not make any enquiry from Dr. Grieve before I got out the summons. Before I got the summons, I telegraphed Mr. LeMessurier, Assistant Collector of Customs, asking him whether duty had been paid on a shipment of guns brought to St. Anthony in the previous September or thereabouts. Frank Lewis told me they had been brought in about that time. I sent the telegram a couple of days before I took out the summons. I have no copy of the telegram. I got a reply from Mr. LeMessurer saying, "No duty paid." I am not sure if these were the exact words but they were to that effect. I received the telegram the day before I got out the summons. I was present at the court the next day. Dr. Grieve appeared. We had Cumby there as a witness. I do not remember what objection Dr. Grieve made for sure, something about the wrong date on the summons, but he got the Magistrate to postpone the case. He had his typewriter-girl there taking down everything that was said. Magistrate Penney was not very pleased with the goings on, no more was I. I finally agreed to the postponement.

After that I came to St. John's myself during the first week of September or thereabouts. I reported the case to the Assistant Collector and the Minister of Customs. I left the matter in their hands. They never notified me no further, but they corroborated the statement that duties had not been paid. They never took any proceedings after that as far as I know.

I have found the officials of the Mission free and open in regard to Custom matters and I never knew them to try and conceal anything from me.

CHAPTER 36

John Grieve on Stand

O n October 24, Dr. John Grieve was examined by Mr. Dunfield and stated under oath:

I am a medical practitioner, M.B., Ch. B. of Edinburgh University 1904, a native of Scotland. I came to Newfoundland to join this Royal National Mission in the year 1906. I have been in service as medical officer on the Labrador from 1906 to the fall of 1916, during which time I was chiefly stationed at Battle Harbour, Labrador. I also spent fifteen months at Harrington, and two short periods of one to two months at St. Anthony. I was appointed secretary and business manager for the International Grenfell Association in December 1916 and still occupy that position.

The IGA is a corporate body registered under the Newfoundland Companies Act. It occupies the position of a holding and spending organization.

The Royal National Mission holds the title to all the properties in Newfoundland. The Medical Superintendent is Dr. Wilfred Grenfell and I am the Secretary and Business Manager.

It is a condition of the organizations of both central and subsidiary corporations that no member of them can derive any profit or advantage either directly or indirectly from his connection with them.

The subscriptions from Newfoundland are $6000 for the year 1916, made up as follows:

Government Grant.............................. $4000
Subscriptions from Nfld Association............... $1000
Government Grant for Pelley's Island Hospital... $1000
Total $6000

With that said, Your Honour, I will now proceed to give my evidence in relation to matters raised by other witnesses:

Mr. Piccott: In his evidence he says that in a certain case a woman would not sell some bakeapple berries to him on the grounds that if she did not sell them to the Mission, they would cut her off from getting anything else from them. As regards to this, I may say that I do not recall the particular case itself, but such an option on the woman's part would be absolutely contrary to the principles and practice of the Mission. Never to my knowledge has there ever been an attempt to coerce people to sell to the Mission in preference to someone else. We would rather extend then curtail the peoples' opportunities of disposing of their goods to advantage.

Mr. Walter B. Grieve: In his evidence he says that three or four years ago I sent a telegram which appeared in the Boston newspapers stating that the people on the Labrador were in a state of starvation and that this was an untrue statement. The explanation of this incident is as follows: I sent a telegram to the Colonial Secretary reading as follows: Dated April 29th 1911. "Colonial Secretary, St. John's. Sir: People from Battle Harbour to Cartwright will starve unless flour comes soon. No flour at Battle or Cartwright. Can you send steamer north. Send twenty barrels by "Home"(coastal boat).

This telegram correctly represents the state of affairs on the Labrador at that time. On the same date I sent a telegraph to Dr. Grenfell, who was then staying in the United States, in care of our office address in New York, as follows:
"People starving on the coast. Have wired Government. When can I see you at St. John's?"
That was a private telegram to Dr. Grenfell. It was opened by the Lady Secretary who passed it over to a representative of the Associated Press, which she had no right to do. That is how the publication came about. As long as she was alive we were unwilling to defend ourselves by laying the blame on her. But as

she is since deceased, the statement can do her no injury. The Government sent the *"Prospero"* (coastal boat) with supplies in the middle of May as far as Hawks Harbour, which relieved the situation. I sent my telegram after ascertaining from the Hudson Bay Company at Cartwright and from Baine Johnston's agent at Battle Harbour that there indeed was no flour available. After that the Agent asked me as a Magistrate to protect him from having people breaking into his stores in search of provisions. The clergyman at Battle Harbour, the Rev. T. Gardiner, had actually asked me to take a schooner and go to the French shore in search of food. Before the supplies arrived some of the people in the vicinity of Cartwright were living on muscles. On my return trip from Cartwright to Battle Harbour I saw no less then thirteen cases of well-marked scurvy brought about by lack of food in addition to several incipient cases of the same disease.

Mr. Walter B. Grieve in his evidence says that four or five years ago the Grenfell Association through his generosity imported in his steamer from England, freight-free, fifteen tons of salt, it was Carrickfergus salt from Ireland, an experiment. He said he does not know if it was used for the fishery or not. I may explain this incident as follows: I saw the salt landed from Baine Johnston's steamer. I heard Dr. Grenfell tell Mr. Croucher to give this salt out to the people to see if it would be as good in the curing of codfish as Cadiz salt. I know that Mr. Croucher gave the salt to the fishermen, every last grain of it. Not one pound was sold for money or exchanged for anything.

Mr. Walter Baine Grieve in his evidence stated that at the annual meeting of the Grenfell Institution in New York Dr. Grenfell admitted that he had been mixed up with cooperative stores and he promised to sever his connection forthwith. In relation to this incident the facts are as follows: Both Dr. Grenfell and I interested ourselves in the cooperative stores at the request of the people to the extent of taking a small number of shares and giving advice. I also acted for some time as Secretary for the Cape Charles Store without renumeration.

At the meeting of the Association in New York in December 1915 a complaint was received from Mr. Grieve against the establishment of this store within three miles of Battle Harbour. After some discussion the meeting passed the following resolution: "That the Secretary notify Dr. Grieve that it is the express desire of the International Board that he sever his connection with the Cape Charles cooperative store, not later than the first day of May 1916 and as much earlier as can be done in justice to the people. I accordingly held the Secretaryship until about September when the new Secretary and manager was established and I withdrew. At that time I resigned my Secretaryship and transferred my shares. Dr. Grenfell transferred his also at the same time. Subsequently to that, the Medical Staff on the Labrador met and passed a resolution to the effect that they considered that they should not be debarred from assisting in any movement, which they considered calculated in improving the condition of the people, in as a large proportion of the disease with which they had to deal was caused by the lack of a proper quantity and quality of food. This resolution was brought up at the meeting of the Board held in New York in September 1916 which I attended. After considerable discussion the meeting finally passed the following resolution:

"RESOLVED that in the opinion of this board the resident physician at Battle Harbour should be left to understand that he is free to give such advice and council to the residents of the neighbourhood who seek his advice as will in his judgment best tend to conserve their interests in connection with the Cape Charles cooperative store on condition that he shall not involve the Mission in any financial or other obligations and on the further condition that he be not allowed to interest himself financially in the undertaking except in so far as is necessary to entitle himself to the privilege of attending stockholders' meetings."

This resolution represented the present policy of the Association as regards to both myself and all other servants of the Mission. I have adhered to this resolution strictly; and I contend that I have an absolute personal right to advise any person upon any matter of business or otherwise.

The same contention would apply to Dr. Grenfell and any other official.

Mr. W. B. Grieve in his evidence says that last year an order drawn from his firm by his agent Croucher at Battle Harbour in favour of the institution was questioned and upon inquiry it was found to represent goods sold whereupon the collector of customs made the Mission pay duty. The order was to pay for codfish put in either by the Grenfell Association or the cooperative store. This I may say entirely misrepresents the incident which was as follows: The cooperative store did not exist at that date. The incident occurred in the fall of 1915 just after I had returned to Battle Harbour from Harrington. I learned that the supply of dry fish for the Hospital had already been bought. Several men with large families came to me and asked me for clothes, wishing to give fish in return. I told them that I could not do so, seeing that we had already enough for the Hospital. A day or two later our Hospital man, Samuel Acreman, informed me that Mr. Croucher would take fish from the people crediting the Mission accounts for the value of the fish, if I would let the people have the clothes. I then saw Mr. Croucher and as in my own mind the transaction seemed doubtful I hesitated to give consent that day. A day or two later I saw Mr. Croucher again and after some discussion and after receiving his assurance that as far as he saw the transaction was fair and above board, I consented to allow the fish to be bought in this way. When the Mission accounts came to be made up, there was a balance in favour of the Mission of about ninety dollars of which I received an order drawn out in the name of the International Grenfell Association. I took this order to St. John's and handed to the late Secretary of the Association, Mr. A. Sheard. Mr. Sheard immediately raised the question as regards customs and he went to Mr. LeMessurier about it. Mr. LeMessurier decided that the transaction was irregular and that duty required to be paid on the amount indicated on the order. I myself saw Mr. LeMessurier and discussed the matter with him. Duty was paid and the incident closed. The matter was not discovered by the Customs but was brought to their attention by Mr. Sheard.

Mr. John Maddock in his evidence says that on one occasion in October some of his crew got money from him which he heard they were going to spend at the Mission for clothes and that he afterwards saw some clothes which they said they had got from the Mission for cash. I would explain this as follows: All members of the staff and employees are given to understand most emphatically that no clothing is to be sold for cash. Of this particular incident the men probably bought the clothes from people who had received them in payment for labor or produce. We have known two cases in the past 10 years where people have sold clothes and because of it were barred from the privilege of obtaining clothing as punishment.

Dr. Grenfell and others have referred in their evidence to the question of fees at the Hospital. I desire to emphasize the special features of our system. No patient is compelled to pay. No patient is refused treatment because he is unable to pay. We have worked out the cost per day of hospital care per patient and we point out to the patient what the cost of the treatment he has received has been and suggest to him that he is under a moral obligation to pay if he can afford it according to his means. The payment is thus voluntary but there has been at work a process of education as a result of which the payments this year at St. Anthony alone already exceed the aggregate receipts at all hospitals last year.

William Belbin of Battle Harbour says in his evidence that I refused to attend a child of his who was suffering from measles. I stated that my reason for this was that an epidemic of measles had just broken out. With a hospital full of patients I had to think of them and not bring measles back to the hospital, where more patients would have been affected with the chance mortality would possibly be great. The same thing happened with Michael Grady's first child, but I attended his second child because by that time measles had broken out in the hospital.

Mr. J. T. Croucher in his evidence mentions the Chubbs man suffering from tuberculosis that wasn't admitted to the hospital at Battle Harbour and died in his boat in the spring of 1915. The reason the man was refused admission to the hospital was due to lack of nurses at that time.

The hotel was built with duty free goods and sold to John Newell on condition he operates it and if he sold it duty would be paid to Customs at that time.

Dr Grieve gave evidence on his time on the Labrador and his relationship with the cooperative store and his efforts to help any way he could to better the conditions of the liviers. He said he never meant to take business away from Baine Johnston and Co.

In reference to the clothing Dr. Grieve produced an itemized list of the amounts of clothing imported during 1916 of $2853.75. He said some of that would be toys and probably surgical supplies and the value he came up with was purely guesswork. Valuation wasn't needed as it comes in duty free.

Sworn before me at St. John's this 25th of October 1917

Signed John Grieve

Before Commissioner Robert Squarey

CHAPTER 37

More from Grieve

The further examination of Dr. Grieve took place on the 29th day of October in St. John's 1917 by Mr. Dunfield. Grieve stated as follows:

In the fall of 1911 there was a stock of guns at the cooperative store: Springfield rifles an old U.S.A. model caliber corresponding to 45-70 Winchester. I suggested to Dr. Grenfell that the Labrador men be allowed the opportunity of purchasing these guns for shooting seals or caribou, seeing that the price was reasonable. That same fall twenty guns were sent by the cooperative store at St. Anthony to Battle Harbour and I placed them in the hands of Isaac Cumby to be sold by him for the cooperative store at a 10 percent commission. During the winter he sold them all and passed the money over to me in August 1912, $140.00 less 10% commission. The money was then passed over to Dr. Grenfell who gave a receipt for the same on behalf of the cooperative store. I now produce and show to the commission the receipt from Dr. Grenfell. As these goods came from the cooperative store, I took it for granted that duty had been paid on them. I had no personal knowledge of the importation, duty, or the entry. Battle Harbour is about sixty miles from St. Anthony and at that time there was no telephone between the two places.

On the 30th of August 1912, a summons was served on me at 9 o'clock at night to appear in court the following day at twelve o'clock before Magistrate Penney to answer for a breach of Sec 96 of the Customs Act. I had no means of knowing at that time whether duty had been paid or not, nor of getting into communication with Dr. Grenfell or with St. Anthony, except by

letter or a special trip across which might take a long time. I
therefore appeared in Court and in order to obtain time made the
objection that the Customs Officers had not the authority from the
Receiver General to take the prosecution under the Customs Act
Sec. 115, as I understood it. I was of the opinion that the
Magistrate and the Customs Officer were both absolutely hostile
to me. The Magistrate was a man who had been in business in Red
Bay and had told me the day before the establishment of the
cooperative stores at Red Bay had destroyed his business. The
case was postponed when I stated these facts. The case was
subsequently dropped when the facts came to light that duty had
been paid by the cooperative store as per entry No.8 St. Anthony
Sept. 26, 1910 regarding rifles of the U.S.A. Army Springfield
type. I also put in receipt given by Isaac Cumby dated Sept. 19th
1912 for 10 percent commission on sale of twenty guns at $7.00 a
piece for the cooperative store at St. Anthony.

Examined further by Mr. Emerson the witness said:

This letter that I produce from Mr. Simms is dated Sept. 19th
1917. I had a previous letter from Mr. Simms but I cannot find it.
According to that letter the declared value of the guns was $105.00
and the duty paid was $36.75.

Re-examined by Mr. Dunfield the witness said:

The difference between the importation price and the sale
price would be accounted for by freight and the cooperative stores
profit. The price was set by the cooperative store not by me or Dr.
Grenfell.

Sworn before me at St. John's aforesaid this 29th day of
October, Anno Domini 1917

Signed John Grieve before Commissioner Robert G. Squarey

So ended the enquiry.

CHAPTER 38

Squarey Report

On Nov. 1, 1917, Judge Squarey submitted his report regarding the commission he had been issued Aug. 1, 1917, to Sir W. H. Horwood, administrator of the Government of Newfoundland

Squarey began by saying that based on the petition signed by the fish merchants - John Rorke & Son, William Duff & Sons, J.J. Maddock, Joseph Udell & Sons, Baine Johnston & Company, R.D. McRae & Sons and James Cron- and from evidence given by witnesses he'd examined during the just concluded enquiry, he had learned:

"That a considerable amount of misunderstanding had arisen with regard to certain aspects of the work performed by the International Grenfell Association, with the chief cause of dissatisfaction originating from the inauguration of cooperative stores by Dr. Grenfell. Resentment had grown out of the manner in which Dr. Grenfell had described conditions in the north of Newfoundland and on the coast of Labrador, when lecturing in the United States and elsewhere, and there was criticism as to the manner in which facilities granted by the Customs Act were availed of by the International Grenfell Association. It will therefore be necessary to consider the evidence in relation to the different aspects of the work of the International Grenfell Association separately and under their different heads, so that a clear and intelligible view may be taken of its work, and any question arising out of this petition considered in the proper place."

He then proceeded to look at (1) the medical work of the Mission (at hospitals in St. Anthony, Battle Harbour, Forteau, and Pilley's Island; (2) the philanthropic work carried out by the Mission (including an orphanage, school, public library, and industrial school in St. Anthony); (3) the religious aspect of the Mission (he noted clergy of all denominations voluntarily and gladly offered testimony of their appreciation of the treatment and courtesy extended to them by the Mission and no one was ever compelled to attend services) and (4) the cooperative stores.

Squarey ended up praising Grenfell's work, and when it came to the cooperative stores he said during his whole investigation he was unable to discover any connection between the International Grenfell Association and the cooperative stores. He stated:

"The cooperative stores were inaugurated by Dr. Grenfell many years ago in the interests of the people to combat, as is alleged, the excessive prices charged at that time by the floating traders, and other mercantile concerns doing business on the coast. According to the evidence taken before me it appears that Dr. Grenfell advanced the money to start these stores in the first instance and it also appears that he personally lost heavily in so doing through bad management on the part of the original managers. There is no evidence that Dr. Grenfell charged interest on the money he loaned, so that the principal involved has been lost to him. His share in the transaction would appear to be much worry and heavy loss. The cooperative stores have since been established on a sound financial basis. In the majority of cases the shares in these stores are owned by the fishermen themselves and they value they so highly that no person residing outside their immediate vicinity can obtain a share under any circumstances. It is plainly manifest that old usages on the coast must give way to modern methods or go under."

Squarey also said he had examined Dr. Grenfell concerning lectures he gave in America and elsewhere. He noted that Grenfell had emphatically denied the charge made by the fish merchants that he had said the population of northern Newfoundland and Labrador were mainly paupers.

When all was said and done Squarey concluded:

"I find after examining sixty witnesses and having made a careful and diligent investigation that the petitioners have failed to prove their contentions."

He said he also found that "the cooperative stores of the coast are not affiliated in any way with the International Grenfell Organization, nor connected with its operations, that with one exception (St. Anthony) it has not appeared that a single share is owned by any member of the Association. It has been shown to my satisfaction that the shares held by Dr. Grenfell in the St. Anthony stores never yielded him any interest or profit but on the contrary entailed much loss until the stores were re-organized and that he is now gradually divesting himself of them in the form of presents to deserving recipients and protégés of his. No breach of the Customs Act has ever been proved. I have been unable to find any justification for the statement in paragraph seven of the petition presented to the Legislature by the eight firms first hereinbefore referred to. I am of the opinion that Dr. Grenfell's reply to my question and his denial to the charge made against him of stigmatizing the people of northern Newfoundland and Labrador as paupers are entitled to the fullest credence."

Squarey's recommendations to the Newfoundland Government:

"For the future peace and harmony which should exist between the business men of northern Newfoundland and Labrador and the International Grenfell Association, I recommend that all clothing imported by the International Grenfell Association except such as is imported for the personal use of the members of the staff, who now have the right to import their personal effects duty free, should pay duty and the Government should make a rebate annually of the amount thus collected. This would, in my opinion, not only tend to the more accurate valuation of the clothing distributed to the people for services and goods supplied to the Association, but would remove any feeling that there is unfair competition. Dr. Grieve, the Secretary at St. John's of the International Grenfell Association, at my request, submitted a schedule of the amount of clothing imported by the Association during the year 1915. He stated that the valuation as given on the Free Entry Form for the information of the Customs amounted to $2,853. This free entry of clothing is a burning sore and a source of constant friction and bitterness between the Association and the businessmen of Newfoundland and Labrador, and the cause of this friction must be removed before friendly relations and peace and harmony are possible between them. If ways and means can be devised to effect this improvement I believe that all parties would work together for the well-being and comfort of the resident population and the prosperity of the whole coast."

Epilogue

On November, 10, 1917, Judge Robert Squarey submitted a bill to the Newfoundland Government for acting as Commissioner in the International Grenfell Association Enquiry.

He stated that his bill was for conducting an enquiry and taking evidence at Carbonear, Harbour Grace, St. Anthony, Battle Harbour, Cape Charles,Forteau, Flowers Cove, Quirpon and St. John's, and along the coast from St. Anthony to Greenspond.

The bill was also for visiting hospitals in St. Anthony, Battle Harbour, Forteau and Pilley's Island, and cooperative stores at St. Anthony, Battle Harbour, Cape Charles and Flowers Cove and reporting on same.

The dates he'd worked were Aug. 30 to Nov. 5, 1917, a total of 67 days. The rate was $10 per day, for a total of $670.

On December 12, Squarey wrote the Deputy Colonial Secretary asking if he would kindly tell him why he had not yet been paid for his services.

On January 25, 1918, the Acting Colonial Secretary sent Squarey a letter saying the Executive Government had ordered he be paid the sum of $400 in full settlement of his services in connection with the International Grenfell Association Enquiry.

On January 30, Squarey submitted a revised bill for 54 days at $10 per day for a total of $570. In this bill he excluded Sundays. He noted in an accompanying letter to the Acting Colonial Secretary that he had been a stipendiary magistrate for early 35 years and was then the senior stipendiary magistrate in the Colony.

He said he'd served on other commissions and his re-numeration was always $10 per day.

"I venture to state that never before in the history of the Colony has such an amount of work and knocking about been accompanied by such a small expense," he stated with indignation.

He went on to note that during his absence from home his out of pocket expenses amounted to nearly as much as he was being offered. He said if he was to get no more than $400 for his services he would always consider that the Government was indebted to him for the balance.

On February 14, 1918, the Deputy Colonial Secretary sent Squarey a letter saying a cheque for $400, the amount the Executive Council allowed in connection with his services, would be forwarded to him.

Final Thought:

Is it any wonder that people didn't trust the fish merchant government? Imagine how the little guy must have suffered when someone like a senior magistrate could not get his just due?

Labrador Family

Tending a patient

Grenfell shelling a lobster

Talking to the children

Battle Habour Hospital

**Dr. and nurse with a
young patient**

Getting around

St. Anthony Orphanage

St. Anthony

Anne,
Grenfell's
beloved wife

ACKNOWLEDGEMENTS

I would like to thank the following people for their assistance in helping me produce this book:

Special thanks go to Gary Newell, Kay Gilbert and all the members of the Grenfell Foundation, the Provincial Archives of Newfoundland and Labrador for providing documents and information concerning the Grenfell era, and staff of the Charles S. Curtis Memorial Hospital.

Iris Fillier, Alvone Sutton, Peter and Jean Stacey for editing.

The following people who helped with research: Ernest Simms, Clyde Patey Sr., Don Loder, Baine and Nancy Pilgrim, Alvone Sutton, Junior Canning, Ceasar Pilgrim, Jack Kennedy, Norm Tucker, Gid Tucker, Rupert Short, Don Manuel, Gerald Hillier, Norman Pilgrim, Nelson Roberts, Cyril Sheppard, Wallace Maynard, Greg Ivany, Sam Compton, Melvin Simms, Carl Pilgrim, Christopher Ellsworth, and Robert Ropson.

Special thanks to my wife Beatrice for reading the manuscript and rearranging layout.

Thank you to Ronald Rompkey for allowing use of his book "Labrador Odyssey: The Journal and Photographs of Eliot Curwen on the Second Voyage of Wilfred Grenfell, 1893" for my story on pages 12 to 16 of this book.

Earl B. Pilgrim

Earl Pilgrim

Best selling author Earl B. Pilgrim was born in St. Anthony in 1939. While serving in the Canadian Army he became involved in the sport of boxing and went on to become Canadian light heavyweight boxing champion.

Earl worked as a Forest Ranger with the Newfoundland and Labrador Forestry Department and as a wildlife protection officer with the Newfoundland Wildlife Service.

He is married to Beatrice (Compton) of Englee. They have four children and live in Roddickton.

Earl and his son Norman have a wilderness lodge in the mountains of the Cloud River on the Great Northern Peninsula of Newfoundland. They do big game hunting for moose, caribou and black bear during the fall, and snowmobiling during winter. They also do trout and salmon fishing during summer. It is to be noted that the area where they hunt and fish is one of the most successful on the island. And, the location where they snowmobile is the finest.

Earl can be reached by calling 709-457-2041
cell 709-457-7071 or email earl.pilgrim@nf.sympatico.ca

Norman can be contacted at 709-457-2451 or
cell 709-457-7117, 709-457-7038.
Web address is www.boughwiffenoutfitters.com